ABOUT THIS BOOK

Every town has stories of its past, and Havenwood Falls is no different. And when the town's residents include a variety of supernatural creatures, those historical tales often become Legends. This is but one . . .

Sequel to *Trapped Within a Wish*, this novella is the continuation of Amani and Nathan's story in Havenwood Falls.

Nathan found more than he bargained for when he came to Havenwood Falls in search of his father's camera, and freeing Amani was only the beginning. Now, they spend time getting to know each other in the town that's become a safe haven, while awaiting the goddess's judgment that will determine Amani and her nefarious sister's fate.

Thoth, the god of wisdom, has been working diligently to find a way to separate the twin djinn females, but Khalida won't go down without a fight. She knows her time is limited and everyone adores her sister over her, but Khalida has discovered a way to show them another version of Amani—a version that could possibly destroy them all.

LEGENDS OF HAVENWOOD FALLS BOOKS

Lost in Time by Tish Thawer

Dawn of the Witch Hunters by Morgan Wylie

Redemption's End by Eric R. Asher

Trapped Within a Wish by Brynn Myers

Blood and Damnation by Belinda Boring

Fated Beginnings by E.J. Fechenda

Emeline by Katie M. John

Released From a Curse by Brynn Myers

A Pack of Lies by Kallie Ross

Kiss the Ashes by Desiree Lafawn

Hidden Truths by Colleen Nye

Wrath and Retribution by Belinda Boring

Changing Fate by Char Webster

Rise of the Witch Hunters by Morgan Wylie

The Drowning Bride by Seven Jane

Also try the main Havenwood Falls series; the YA line, Havenwood Falls High; the darker, sexier side of town, Havenwood Falls Sin & Silk; and the local supernatural college, Sun & Moon Academy.

Stay up to date at www.HavenwoodFalls.com

ALSO BY BRYNN MYERS

RELEASED FROM A CURSE

A LEGENDS OF HAVENWOOD FALLS NOVELLA

BRYNN MYERS

"They slipped briskly into an intimacy from which they never recovered."
—F. Scott Fitzgerald, *This Side of Paradise*

CHAPTER 1

EGYPT

Thoth checked on Khalida and found her sleeping soundly. She looked so innocent, but as he found out earlier, looks can be deceiving. Khalida had yet to calm since arriving here. At first, she'd been vicious, and he'd assumed it was a result of being contained within the Prison of Asria, a watcher's vessel used only by the elite guard. It had the finest accommodations and was more than adequate to house any djinn, most certainly a betrayer the likes of Khalida, but Thoth opted to try to earn her trust by offering her a choice—stay in the vessel or move to a home of her choosing. Khalida had of course picked the latter, but there was a catch Thoth had neglected to mention. The *home* would have invisible walls, allowing him to observe her every move. It was for his research. He needed to know everything he could about her. His frustration had been that he wouldn't be able to observe Amani too.

"I'm tired of living in this glass house. I'd rather be in the prison," Khalida raged, her fists banging the clear glass.

"The choice was made. You will live within the boundaries," Thoth replied coldly.

Khalida began to change, her skin paling as her eyes turned opaque. Silver hieroglyphs appeared on her arms and chest, and her raven locks turned stark white. Khalida was enraged, exactly as Thoth hoped she'd be, when he took a sample of her blood. He held his palm outstretched, and silver liquid began to flow from her to him, incensing her even more. The blood easily passed through the barrier between them and swirled in a tornadic twist, hovering just above Thoth's hand.

"That should be enough this time," he said as he willed the blood into a vial on the table behind him.

Khalida had not felt any pain—Thoth had made sure of it when he extracted her life force—but she raged on nonetheless. He quickly became annoyed with her tantrum and snapped his fingers. In an instant, Khalida returned to her human appearance and began to float midair. Thoth used his thoughts to move her through the air until she was hovering above her bed. Gently laying her down, he moved the blanket placed at the end of her bed to cover her.

"Sleep well, djinn."

Thoth thought back to when Khalida was a young girl, before the djinn in her matured and she became the force of destruction and chaos she was today. She was a quiet child, introspective and curious. Some called her aloof, but Thoth saw she was always thinking, always planning. Khaldun had been assigned to them as a watcher the day of their change—a mistake too late to remedy at this point, but a mistake nonetheless. A watcher is only there to observe and report. Action is only taken when commanded by one of the gods, himself included. Amani and Khalida had been different, though, and while the normal course of action was taken to keep guard over their upbringing, Thoth had wanted to observe the twins firsthand. He'd never wanted to appear as the god he was and only have them respond to him in reverence. Instead, he appeared as a servant working in the house. It gave him a chance to see them in a relaxed atmosphere, where they didn't feel as though they were being monitored. They were, after all, children growing up in a human world, no one ever suspecting what lay just beneath the surface.

Amani was warm and thoughtful, easy to approach, while Khalida was cool and cautious, wanting to understand people's intentions before she allowed them in. At one of Thoth's impromptu visits, he posed as a guard. He watched as the girls came down the hall, Amani carrying a doll and Khalida a familiar rectangular box filled with dice —Senet, a favorite game among children and adults. When one of the maids tripped and fell as she came down the stairs, Amani rushed to her side, asking what she could do to help, while Khalida stared at them, arms crossed and agitated.

"Will our breakfast be late now?"

"Khalida," Amani scolded. "Syrah has hurt her ankle. We can get our own meal."

Khalida glared at them for a moment before she turned and walked away. Thoth broke character as a guard and asked her what happened, even though he'd seen it all play out from across the room.

Khalida's response was swift. "She was clumsy, and now I have to suffer."

"How are you suffering?"

Khalida glared up at him. "What concern is it of yours?"

Thoth shook his head and went back to his stance as a guard as she walked away, not once turning back to see if Amani and Syrah were still seated on the floor. This was just one of many examples over the years of how they were two sides of the same coin— opposites in every way. Light and dark separated, but then again, they were born of an argument between Sekhmet and Shu. It could just be that the twins were elements of their makers' personalities, and the differences between them had nothing to do with one another at all. All Thoth knew was he had much to learn about them, and what he'd hoped would be easy had become a challenge, a riddle to solve.

Thoth made his way over to his lab and began to process Khalida's silver blood. He knew one of these times he'd find a unique marker that would show him the path to separating Amani and Khalida. He was just missing one piece, and once he had that, the process could begin. However, this missing link was elusive. How connected and linked were they? They were twins, yes, but they shared so much more. He needed to find out their secrets.

Khalida began to moan, and Thoth turned to understand why she would be awake. He'd put her to sleep, and she should be down until he chose to wake her. Khalida was writhing on the bed and tugging at her linen sheath. Thoth turned to grab a vial to extract more of her blood to try to identify the cause, but when he did, he noticed the blood he'd taken earlier was changing—reacting to something. Thoth took a closer look and noticed gold flecks shimmering within Khalida's mercurial blood. He turned back to Khalida and grinned when she called out Nathan's name. This was it, the moment he'd been waiting for.

Thoth held out his palm and summoned more of her blood as she continued to writhe in ecstasy. This time her blood swirled in his palm, not in a silver vortex but a twisted gold and silver ladder. Was Amani the same? He needed to know.

Khalida awoke in a spark of light and stood before Thoth. She was still trapped behind his invisible cage, but awake nonetheless.

"What have you done to me?"

"Nothing. You woke of your own accord," Thoth replied as he placed the blood he'd just received from her into a crystal container. "I have no idea how you've managed it, but I will uncover it soon enough."

"RELEASE ME!"

Thoth snapped his fingers, and Khalida's screams were silenced. She continued to rage, but at least he didn't have to hear it. Thoth moved back to his vials and the container holding Khalida's blood—correction, Amani and Khalida's blood—and went to work on finding the solution, now that he had the pieces to the puzzle.

CHAPTER 2

HAVENWOOD FALLS

*A*s the morning light spilled into the cabin, Amani began to wake. She was in Nathan's arms, their bodies intertwined, naked and unabashed. The covers on the bed were tousled, and the cool mountain air was blowing in from the slightly open window.

"You are so beautiful in the morning," Nathan said as he twirled one of the curls near her face. "I mean, you're beautiful every morning, but now, here in my arms . . ."

"I thought the only way I could feel another person's emotions was to be in contact with their blood or life force, but with you," she paused, "I've never felt a connection so deeply."

"Amani, I've spent my entire life hiding my emotions. I assumed it was better than letting anyone in to see my pain. Losing my parents at an early age was hard. Yes, I had Lillian and I'm grateful for her, but I chose to bury myself in my work instead of experiencing life." He brushed back the hair from her face. "Then, in the process of trying to find closure, I found you."

Amani reached for Nathan's hand. "We found each other, it seems."

"You have stolen my heart."

"I didn't mean to steal anything," she protested innocently.

"Not in the actual sense." Nathan chuckled. "I mean, you've made it so I will never be able to be with another. I am yours and yours alone, Amani."

She leaned in closer, their lips inches apart. "I've been learning about what it means to love. A parent loves a child, and the child loves the parent. I thought I loved Khalida, but I was wrong about what her love meant. What does it mean to love someone other than your family?"

Nathan pulled her closer until their lips touched.

"It feels like this," he said as he kissed her. He deepened their kiss and held her gently in his arms.

Amani pulled back after a few moments. "I think I like love."

"I think I like love, too."

The two spent the next hour talking and making love. It was glorious to be in perfect communion with what had become the other half of their souls. They had an inexplicable connection, and if it wasn't love, then love surely didn't exist.

"In your eyes, Amani, I see the hope of a thousand futures, and my only wish is that I get to spend at least one of them with you."

Amani placed her hand on the side of Nathan's face. "It is I who hopes to spend more than that with you."

Nathan rose with a final peck to the tip of her nose. "And that we will, but first, it's time for me to meet Calla Lily."

Amani smiled, acknowledging his commitment, then watched as he sauntered to the bathroom. Upon hearing the water of the shower, she turned to gaze out the window as another deer passed in front of the cottage they'd been offered outside Whisper Falls Inn. It was small and quaint and served as the perfect place for the two of them to stay while Thoth and the goddesses figured out a solution to break the link between her and Khalida. The views of the mountains were amazing, and of all the places they could've ended up, they were lucky it was here. It had been a long time since Amani had seen animals roaming about or trees swaying when the wind blew before a summer rain. Everything about Havenwood Falls seemed like a dream.

The days following the incident in the square had been hectic to say the least. The supernatural residents were now aware of the powerful djinn they had living in their town and were reluctant to embrace Nathan and Amani as a result. Amani, however, wanted nothing more than to meet each and every one of them. She wanted to learn about what made them unique and if any of them were like her. Calla Lily explained that it might take time and them getting to know her before the tension would ease and they became welcoming.

"You simply need to show everyone the Amani we know, and not the djinn Roman has informed them about," Calla Lily had said.

"But I will not harm them," Amani had replied.

"They don't know that—yet," Calla Lily had insisted.

However, time was the one word Amani didn't want to hear. She'd lost too much of that and missed out on so many experiences when she was bound to the camera and the canopic jars. Now all she wanted to do was make up for it. She spent most days trying to be as normal as possible, which for her was hard. Amani couldn't turn off the immense power coursing through her veins, and yet all she wanted was to be like everyone else. She wanted to show not only the goddesses and Thoth, but Nathan, too, that she could make this work—that she could live in the human world and not hurt anyone—but not using her powers was a work in progress.

Nathan and Calla Lily were trying to help her to understand her powers and what it meant to be a djinn. Calla Lily had found some ancient family tombs, but they were of little to no help, considering Amani and Khalida were unlike others of their kind. The three of them thought if Amani could learn to control the energy surging through her, she'd be all right. However, whenever she used her powers, the Court of the Sun and the Moon, the supernatural leaders of this town, sensed the surges and insisted on boundaries until they could feel comfortable with her abilities. They'd convened a meeting and collectively decided to mark her with a magical brand to try to bind her powers, or at least subdue them. Their attempt ended in failure.

Amani's hieroglyphs began to glow, and it was clear the Court would have to find another way. She tried to explain she wasn't angry, that the symbols were a reaction to the intense magic they were wielding, but they weren't willing to risk it. Instead, they asked her to never use her magic without consulting one of the members of the Court. Mihail Petran, who owned the inn and was also on the Court, along with his wife Irina and sister-in-law Madame Luiza, had volunteered to keep a close eye on her—not that there was much to see.

Whenever Amani wasn't communing with nature, she was reading to learn about modern society.

For all the years she was bound to the canopic jars, she wasn't without education. Thoth had given them a library full of ancient texts and information about the beings who roamed the worlds, along with languages and customs for every culture. It was available to her and Khalida, but Khalida didn't care to learn about things she'd never experience. Learning about the outside world only made her acrimonious, so she refused to ever read them, but thankfully, Amani had, and now she had a wealth of knowledge.

Amani already knew something about every being living in Havenwood Falls, but only had snippets of information for some. Which was why she was so excited when she'd encounter one in person. She wanted to ask them questions and compare notes to what she already knew about their race. With that in mind, Amani caught sight of more movement outside the cottage and quickly dressed, running barefoot out the front door.

CHAPTER 3

*T*ilting his head from side to side, Nathan stretched the tight muscles as he continued to dry off. Spotting Amani outside, her golden curls glinting in the sun as she knelt next to a tree, he wondered what she was doing. However, if he'd learned anything during the past few weeks, it would be a waste to assume anything other than she was communing with nature and connecting to the energy within Havenwood Falls. At first, he had no clue what she was talking about, but after a few examples and some help from her and Calla Lily, he too could feel the electrical buzz. Calla Lily referred to it as "magic in the air," while Amani seemed to feel it from every living thing. Either way, Havenwood Falls had become a special place for them both.

Nathan took one last look at Amani before continuing to get dressed. He was set to meet with Calla Lily shortly. She'd left word that she received a letter and they needed to talk about it. He'd wondered what it could be about but quickly dismissed it, since no one other than Lillian knew he was still here. He'd called her a few days after the showdown in the town square to say he was going to be extending his stay a bit longer—that he was enjoying the tranquility of the mountains. Lillian had of course questioned him, but then told him to enjoy his much-needed vacation.

"I'll expect you in a week then," Lillian had quickly stated, then said she loved him and hung up. It was, after all, a long-distance call.

"Hi," Nathan said as Amani walked into the room.

"There was an angel outside, but when I went to talk to her, she vanished, so I talked to the trees instead."

Nathan kissed her cheek. "And did you learn anything today?"

"Only that the trees love being close to the pond and close to the aether."

"Aether?"

"Yes, it's a part of the universe—part of everything. The aether was put there many years ago by a witch—a Howe witch to be exact."

Nathan put on his waistcoat and buttoned the buttons. "That sounds interesting."

"It was. She was beautiful and powerful."

"More powerful than you?"

"I am uncertain. I could only feel her magic through the land, but based on that, it is possible," Amani said as she found a vase for the handful of wildflowers she was holding in her hand.

"You don't normally pick the flowers."

"No, they were a gift from the pixies."

"They're beautiful."

"You are ready to go?" she asked as Nathan sat to put on his shoes.

"Yes, I'm headed to see Calla Lily now. Would you like to come?"

"No, but I'd love to walk with you until you start to head past the inn. Madame Luiza offered to show me how to cook food. Maybe soon I can cook for us here." Amani beamed.

"I'd like that," Nathan said, reaching for his pocket watch. "Are you ready to go?"

"Yes," she said as she picked up the vase of wildflowers. "I want to give these to Irina."

"I think she'll love them," he replied, latching the door to the cottage.

Nathan dropped off Amani and made his way down the cobbled street until he reached Calla Lily's shop. He moved to open the door, but was halted when it swung toward him. Nathan stood face to face with Roman Bishop, who glared at him before walking past without a word.

"Good morning to you too, Roman," Nathan said as he shook his head and looked at Calla Lily standing in the doorway. "What's his problem today?"

"Well, despite that being his normal demeanor, he's especially agitated because I won't help him find out more about the djinn race and their abilities."

"Why does he want to know so badly?"

"Because he saw her strength. And Roman always wants to align himself with power. He was asking me about ancient texts, but unfortunately I'm fresh out," Calla Lily shrugged.

"Is he always like this with visitors to Havenwood Falls? I mean, does he always want to investigate the supernaturals who visit?" Nathan leaned in close and whispered.

"No, not necessarily investigate, but after what happened, I'm sure he sees Amani as a threat, and therefore the research he's doing on the djinn species is more intense. Amani and Khalida are unique, and I'm sure he just wants to know all he can about his foes."

Nathan's brow arched. "Amani is not his foe."

"I know that, but since she refuses to give him information regarding the Prison of Asria and why it can contain a djinn, he's taking it personally."

"Well, he needs to get over it," Nathan snapped. "We'll be gone soon enough."

Calla Lily frowned. "He's the only one who won't miss you two. Madame Luiza, Irina, and I were all talking to Saundra Beaumont about how much fun it is to watch Amani as she experiences the world. She's thousands of years old, but in many ways, she's just a young girl who has the wonder of youth in her favor."

"Yeah, she does. This morning she was talking to the trees."

Calla Lily laughed. "The aspens behind the cottage?"

Nathan nodded. "Apparently, some pixies gave her some flowers."

"Well, this is good news. They are comfortable with her, and we need others to feel the same."

Calla Lily walked to the back of the shop for a moment, returning with a package. It was postmarked to him c/o Calla Lily Mircea.

"What's this?"

"I'm not exactly sure," she said as she pointed to the return address, "but it's from New York."

He scrunched his face. "I sent her a letter after our call to explain everything—well, as much as I could explain, that is. I wonder what she has sent."

"Only one way to find out," Calla Lily said as she handed him a pair of scissors.

Nathan opened the box, and the edge of his lips turned upward into a grin. "She sent some of the parchments I'd been working on before I left."

A customer walked in, and Calla Lily moved out from behind the counter to go help her. It was then that he opened the handwritten letter and pulled his glasses from his vest pocket.

Dear Nathan,

I'm glad you're taking some time for yourself, but we both know all too well you'll be missing your work soon enough. I took the liberty to send you some pages still in need of translation. I hope the mountain air and peace and quiet will help clear your mind so you can return to New York fresh and inspired. This is the new start you've so desperately needed now that you have closure with Samuel's camera and journal. I miss you terribly and look forward to seeing you soon.

Love, Lillian

Nathan folded the letter and began to look through the parchments. He'd always wondered what some of the hieroglyphs meant, but now looking at them again, he recognized more of them. He'd seen them recently.

"Look at this. Recognize these?" he asked after Calla Lily said goodbye to her customer.

"Amani has these same markings," Calla Lily gasped.

"This one is fire." He adjusted his glasses. "This one means wind, and this one here is related to Sekhmet." He pointed.

"Could this be about her and Khalida then? About how they were created?"

"Possibly, but why would it be amongst the things I was working on? I had no idea about djinn before I came here."

Calla Lily's brow arched. "That's the thing about fate, Nathan—you can't hide from it. It finds you whether you want it to or not. You were always meant to be here. You and Amani were always meant to be together."

Nathan's eyes went wide. "I wish I understood things the way you do. Being human is a bit of an inconvenience," he laughed. Calla Lily chuckled and bade Nathan farewell, but as he walked back toward the inn, he thought about what she'd said in regards to fate.

With a clear picture of Amani in his mind, he felt as though his life had started with a single letter regarding his father's camera.

"Did you and Calla Lily have a good meeting?" Amani asked, taking notice of the items in his hands.

"Oh!" Nathan said as he jerked back, almost losing his grip on the parchments. "We did," he said, lifting them in his hand. "Lillian sent these."

"I didn't mean to startle you."

"It's all right. I was just thinking about you and then there you were."

"You were thinking about me?"

Nathan smiled. "I'm always thinking about you."

Amani's face lit up. "So, what are they?"

"Stories and mentions of you and Khalida, I think," he replied.

"About us? Why would you have parchments written about Khalida and me?"

"To be honest, I'm not certain, but these were ones sent by the other Egyptologists after my father's disappearance. They were apparently found near your vessel." He moved toward the parlor. "Do you remember me telling you about the jar sitting on a ledge with a barrier of red stones carved like scarabs and a shimmering liquid no one could identify?" Nathan asked, spreading out the parchment on the coffee table. "The one with the mysterious hieroglyphs?"

"Yes, I remember. The ones the night raiders came in and attempted to steal when they were badly burned."

"Yes." He pointed to a line of hieroglyphs. "This here, if I'm reading it correctly, talks of the protective magic surrounding the two jars."

"This references the scarabs. They're colored red to show they were made of carnelian." She pointed to the next. "And this references the mercury."

"That's mercury?"

Amani nodded. "What did you think it was?"

"I thought it represented Hathor, with the circle and half-moon here at the top."

"No, Hathor is here," Amani said, moving down the page a bit. "Oh my, this *is* a reference to Khalida and me."

"Why do you say that? I mean, I am happy to confirm my suspicions, but I'm too curious for you not to clarify it."

"All of these symbols and their descriptions. Sekhmet and Shu are here, along with Hathor and Ma'at. Then, there are the references to silver and gold, fire and ice, darkness and light. All of this here shows how we were made and how we ended up broken." Amani shook her head. "I don't understand. Why would they have our story documented? We were a disgrace and had to be hidden away."

Nathan sighed. "You are not a disgrace, Amani. I think it's more likely that they wrote it down to explain how you two came to be. It's been said many times that you and Khalida are special and nothing is more evidence of that than the power you two wield."

"I suppose so."

"I find it interesting and comforting in equal measure," Nathan said, rolling up the parchment and putting it into the leather sleeve.

"Why is that?" Amani asked as Nathan set the container on the settee.

"Calla Lily told me when we first met that sometimes the answers we seek don't always come the way we hope. Sometimes, we find something entirely different. She said that it was important to keep an open mind when it came to the possibilities beyond understanding."

"And how does that apply to Khalida and me being part of the parchment?" she questioned.

"Because if my father had never been in Egypt and been a part of your past, you would never be part of my present and hopefully my future," Nathan said, reaching for her hands and pulling them to his lips. "I think Calla Lily knew what was about to transpire all along, and those words were meant for me to keep an open mind."

Amani blushed. "I guess fate did bring us to this point, and I'll be forever grateful."

CHAPTER 4

*T*he next morning, Nathan was shaving when he heard the front door close. When he walked out of the bathroom with a towel around his neck, his suspenders hanging at his sides, and his undershirt exposed, Amani stared at him curiously.

"What is on your face?"

He laughed. "Shaving cream. You use it to get rid of facial hair you don't want."

"I like your facial hair. Do not use that cream to remove it."

Nathan used the towel to wipe it off and grinned. "Very well. I will keep the whiskers for you."

Amani rushed into his open arms. "I heard the wolves roaming the woods earlier and was up hoping to catch their attention. I would love to talk to one of them. I have so many questions." Amani beamed as Nathan held her close.

"I'm certain you do, but like Calla Lily said, the town is still trying to adjust to you being here. Give them time. I'm sure they'll be happy to talk to you soon," Nathan said as he kissed her forehead.

Amani looked up at him. "The pixies talk to me, but that angel is still elusive. Are you hungry? I made breakfast."

"You did?"

"Yes," she beamed. "I made oatmeal."

Nathan's brows furrowed. "How'd you learn to make oatmeal?"

"Madame Luiza showed me yesterday," she said as she took Nathan by the hand and led him into the kitchen. "Mine doesn't smell exactly like hers, but I think I did it right."

There on the stove was a large cast iron pot with steam rising. When Amani reached for the spoon to stir it, Nathan knew something was off.

"Amani, honey, what did you put in here?"

"Oats, water, cinnamon, and salt."

Nathan nodded his head. "And what else?"

"Garlic." Amani beamed.

"Ah yes, that's it." Nathan scrunched his nose.

Her face fell. "What is wrong with that? My mother often put garlic in with the breakfast grains."

"We don't really use garlic for breakfast," he said as he tugged his ear, "but I appreciate that you went to the trouble to make food for me. You know you don't have to, right?"

Amani's face fell and her shoulders slumped.

"No, no, no." Nathan said as he brushed the hair from her face and gently caressed her cheek.

"But I failed. Maybe I can't be a human after all."

"I don't think anyone ever expected you to. I know I certainly don't. You're perfect just the way you are."

A smile spread across her face. "Really?"

"Really," Nathan answered. "Besides, why would I ever want you to be a boring human like me when I've seen how amazing you are when you embrace your djinn?"

Amani's face fell again. "It is not good for me to embrace that side of me, Nathan. Not for you and not for those around me. I'm dangerous."

He reached for her hands and pulled them to his lips. "Beautiful and dangerous, yes, but you are good, and more importantly, you are not your sister."

"Khalida is only part of the story, and she wasn't all bad either. She had a good side—a sort of loving side." Amani sighed. "She chose to let the bad rule her—to be different."

"That's what I'm saying. You choose good, and therefore the parts of you that scare you can be controlled."

Amani met Nathan's eyes. "I just hope Thoth finds a solution soon. Then I won't have to worry anymore."

"I'm sure he will. In the meantime, how about we get dressed and head over to the inn for some of Madame Luiza's blueberry jam and biscuits."

Amani nodded. "I do love that jam."

Nathan turned off the burner and used a towel to push the hot pan to the center of the stove. "Best to let that cool before we do anything with it."

Nathan and Amani left the cottage and walked over to the inn, hoping they hadn't missed breakfast. "Do you think there are still some biscuits left? I want a biscuit."

Nathan laughed. "I'm sure Madame Luiza will have extra."

When they rounded the corner and walked into the dining room, the scent of freshly cooked bacon wafted over to them. "Now that is breakfast."

"Nathan," Amani scolded.

"I'm sorry. Garlic and oatmeal are just not a good combination."

"What is this about oatmeal and garlic?" Madame Luiza asked as she headed out of the kitchen.

Amani's face fell, and Nathan scrambled to answer the question without upsetting her any further. "Well, ugh, yeah."

Madame Luiza crossed her arms in front of her chest. "What did you do, Nathan?"

Amani interjected before Nathan could respond. "I made the oatmeal just like you told me to, but I added garlic like my mother used to, and he didn't like it."

Madame Luiza bit back a smile. "Well, garlic is not exactly a good addition, Amani," she said as she put her arm around Amani. "How about we meet again tomorrow and learn something you can use garlic in."

Nathan mouthed, "Thank you."

"You're not off the hook, Nathan," Amani said as she walked toward one of the tables.

"Madame Luiza, you still have biscuits, right?" Nathan whispered.

Madame Luiza laughed. "I have blueberry jam as well, but I doubt that will save you from this, dear."

"Yeah, but a fella can try, right?"

"Flowers might help." She winked.

Nathan and Amani laughed as Madame Luiza brought out their breakfast. Conversation flowed smoothly as they talked to Irina and Madame Luiza about going into Montrose, but things turned somber again when they cautioned against Amani leaving, out of concern for any repercussions with the goddesses or even with Roman and the Court. They agreed it was best for her to stay put until Thoth, Hathor, and Ma'at returned.

Amani turned to face the lobby when the door opened and Roman walked into Whisper Falls Inn, his arrogance leading a few steps ahead of him. Amani caught his eye as she walked out of the dining room and into the parlor. The two glared at one another before Mihail interrupted the nonverbal exchange.

"What can I do for you, Roman?"

"Just stopping by to make sure things are going smoothly. You know, for the town and the Court's safety," he said, casting a glance in Amani's direction.

"Everything is going well. Nathan and Amani have settled in quite nicely. We see them every day."

"You do?" Roman questioned.

Irina came to stand next to her husband. "Yes, Roman. We do," she insisted.

The chime on the door drew all of their attention. There in the doorway stood a man in dungarees and a rugged worn shirt rolled up to mid-forearm.

"Oh good. You're here," Roman said as Sheriff Ric Kasun strode toward them.

"The question is why, Roman. Why did you ask me to join you here?"

Mihail offered his hand. "Good morning, Ric."

"Can I get you a cup of coffee?" Irina asked.

"That would be great. Thank you."

"Are you all done with niceties? I'd like to have a real conversation," Roman snapped.

"Of course, Roman, because the world exists for your needs only, it seems," Ric quipped.

Irina returned with a mug and handed it to Ric. "Madame Luiza said she has a plate waiting for you when you're finished here."

Ric nodded. "I appreciate that. Hopefully this won't take long," he said, taking a sip of the coffee and glaring at Roman over the rim of the mug.

Roman's lip curled into a snarl. "We need to have yet another discussion about our new residents and how they—or she—should be monitored. You may not have been in the square that night, Ric, but that djinn is more of a threat than she appears to be."

"What is your concern? From what I understand, she is doing well here and is no threat to the town or its residents. Unless *you* are feeling threatened, Roman."

The look on Roman's face spoke volumes, and everyone present knew Ric had struck a nerve. However, when Amani entered the room, Roman's tension seemed to amplify—hers too.

"Amani, we'd like to you to meet Ric Kasun," Mihail offered.

Her eyes lit up as he extended his hand in greeting. "You are one of them—one of the wolves I've seen in the woods. I've wanted to meet you. To say hello," she rambled on. "You're beautiful."

Ric cleared his throat. "Um. Thank you?"

"Yes. I've been watching you and the other wolves in the mornings. I've never met any human wolves. I mean, shifters," she said quickly as she glanced over at Irina. "I've been learning more about the people who live here in Havenwood Falls. I hope I haven't offended you."

Ric smiled. "No, not at all. It's nice to meet you as well. Welcome to our town. If you need anything, feel free to reach out to me or my wife, Gaby."

"Thank you. I will do that. I'd love to know more about you and your kind. I transform, too, but not like you."

Roman huffed, and Amani cast her eyes to him in disgust, a few of the hieroglyphs shimmering on her arms and neck. "Why is it that you are here, Roman? I have done nothing to warrant questioning. The little incident of magic was me helping one of the pixies in the forest this morning, nothing more."

"You are not allowed to use your powers within the boundaries of this town," Roman barked. "And it's clear you do not grasp what exactly that means."

"I'm no threat to you or anyone here."

"And how can we be certain of that when you refuse to talk about who and what you are?"

"Is that what this is all about, Roman?" Ric questioned. "Because if it is, Conall saw her this morning doing just as she said—helping. A rabbit became trapped in a briar patch, and she helped free it from the snarl."

Amani arched a brow, and Roman narrowed his eyes at Ric. "No magic means no magic."

Ric took another sip of his coffee and addressed Roman. "I think this is about something more than anyone breaking the rules or laws, and I'm hungry. I don't think we have an issue here." He turned to look at Amani. "Thank you for helping the rabbit. It was an act of mercy and kindness." Ric nodded at Mihail and Irina before walking past the group on his way toward the dining room. "Madame Luiza," he called out.

"Useless as usual," Roman grumbled.

"What is it that you hoped to accomplish, Roman?" Amani asked. "Why do you harbor resentment toward me? I've done nothing to deserve your angst."

"You have the power to destroy even your own kind. It makes you a liability," he said as he moved to leave. "I'm serious about no magic, and I will make certain your sanctuary is revoked if you continue to break the rules."

The moment Roman's hand touched the handle of the door, Amani moved in a blur to stand next to him. "I think you're afraid of me, but again, I am not a threat to you."

Roman glared at her. "You have no intention of listening, do you?" he said, then opened the door and walked out without another word.

Amani turned to Mihail and Irina. "What have I done to make him dislike me so much?"

Irina shook her head. "Don't take it personally. It's just a power trip. If he doesn't control said power, he'll continue to count it as a threat. It's just who he is."

The door chimed again, and Amani spun around, expecting it to be Roman again with another round of rules she was to follow, but instead Calla Lily walked in.

"What's wrong?" she asked, reaching for Amani's hand. "You look upset."

Amani shook her head, doing her level best to control her budding frustration.

Calla Lily's nose crinkled. "Roman was here. Never mind, that explains everything."

Calla Lily, Mihail, and Irina all chuckled as Amani walked back into Nathan's arms. Madame Luiza quickly changed the subject and offered to show Amani how to make chocolate cake. The distraction was just what they needed.

Nathan and Amani both spent the afternoon helping out at the inn, then cleaning up after the dinner service, finally heading back to the cottage once the last dish was put away.

"I think I'll take a bath before I change for bed," Amani said before she rose up on her toes to kiss Nathan on the cheek.

"How about I make us some hot cocoa? I found some sugar and cocoa powder in the cupboard."

"That sounds wonderful."

"Enjoy your bath," he said as he kissed her lips.

Amani didn't take long in the bath, but when she came out, she appeared calm and at ease. Nathan had started a fire, and the wood's crackling was the only sound in the room.

"Feel better?"

"Yes, thank you," she said as she took the mug from Nathan and sat down on the couch beside him.

Amani nodded and took a sip. "This is delicious."

"Nothing fixes things faster than a warm cup of hot cocoa," he said with a grin plastered on his face.

Amani laughed. "Can we give some of this to Roman then?"

"I'll see what I can do."

Amani took one last sip and curled into Nathan's lap. The two of them stayed like that, talking and laughing until the fire died out, then moved to tuck themselves into bed.

Nathan winked at her as he adjusted the covers. "Goodnight, beautiful."

"Goodnight, Nathan."

CHAPTER 5

*N*athan woke to Amani crying out in the middle of the night and bolted out of bed. She wasn't awake, but she was talking in her native tongue. He recognized it from the fight between her and Khaldun. It was the bizarre language the watcher had spoken before he tried to trap Amani. Tears began to stream down her face, and Nathan wasn't sure what to do to help her. He took a step closer and reached for her leg.

"Amani, can you hear me? Wake up."

Hieroglyphs started to glow on her skin, and Nathan took a step back. *Oh no.*

"Sweetheart, you need to wake up," he said as calmly but as urgently as he could. Her djinn symbols cooled from a vibrant gold into a steely grey. "There you go. Can you open your eyes and talk to me?"

Nothing happened. Amani remained motionless. When she hadn't spoken or moved for several moments, Nathan decided the threat of her changing had passed. He moved back to his side of the bed and sat down beside her, placing a hand on her arm. A smile tipped her lips, and she turned toward him.

"I heard your voice. I didn't know where I was, but I heard you calling to me just like you did in the town square to bring my djinn side to heel."

"Where were you?"

"I'm not sure, but I could feel Khalida. I felt her rage and pain."

"Is Thoth hurting her?"

"No, she is free."

"Free?" Panic lit Nathan's eyes.

"Not in the literal sense, but in a cage of sorts—like our canopic jars. She has all she could ever want and need supplied for her."

"Then why the rage and pain?"

"That was for me and the loss of her love, Khaldun."

"You were speaking his language. Did you know that?"

Amani nodded. "She wanted me to know she is still with me despite her entrapment. That she will come for me and take all I care about as payment for my deeds."

Nathan reached for her hand. "But the goddesses and Thoth have her. She can't harm you."

"Not physically. But I will need to do a better job of blocking her."

"Maybe there is something Calla Lily can do to help."

Amani nodded. "Maybe."

"We'll figure out something. We're in this together," he said as he pulled her fingers to his lips and kissed them gently. "Try and get some rest. I'll be right in the other room, okay?"

She met his gaze. "Will you stay with me? I feel better when you're close."

Nathan nodded. "Of course."

Amani moved to lay back down, and Nathan slid in beside her. She shimmied backward until her body melded into his. Nathan smiled and put his arm around her, pulling her closer.

"Amani, you mean everything to me," Nathan whispered, kissing the nape of her neck. "I will go to the ends of the earth to keep you safe and happy."

She turned to look back at him, her eyes speaking all the words her lips refused to utter.

"I may only be human, but there is more than one way to care for you." Nathan pushed the strap of her nightgown over her shoulder and continued to kiss her bare skin. Amani arched her back and moaned as he let his hands roam, following the curves of her body.

Amani fit perfectly against him, and he loved how her skin felt against his. Nathan's body reacted to hers instinctively. He lifted the end of the satin gown up over her hips, exposing her bare bottom.

"I plan on taking my time with every inch of you," he said as he kissed his way up her neck. "Every inch," he crooned, wishing this would never end. He wanted to love her not only in this moment but for the rest of their lives. He never knew love could happen so fast. He'd seen his friends go from single to married in no time flat, but he never thought it would happen to him.

Amani writhed beneath him. She wanted him as much as he wanted her, and that only pushed him further over the edge. When she rolled over and tugged open his shirt, running her hands run up his chest, Nathan sucked in a breath at the feel of her hands on his skin.

"You have my heart," she whispered.

Nathan smiled at her and moved his hand over hers. A warm sensation tingled in her fingertips, and the golden liquid that initiated their whole journey together flowed from her directly into his heart. Nathan winced for a moment, then sighed at her as recollection dawned. He could now feel her emotions, hear her thoughts again, as their connection reignited with another drop of her djinn blood.

The two of them made love again and again, finishing, then starting as if they'd never started to begin with. They were insatiable for one another until they finally wore themselves out. However, a few short hours into their second round of sleep, there was a knock at the door. Nathan grabbed the blanket on the edge of the bed and tied it around his waist in a simple knot that hung at his hips. On the third knock, he opened the door.

Calla Lily sucked in a breath and pursed her lips. "Um okay . . . so it seems like I've intruded. Sorry about this, but we have a problem that needs immediate attention."

"Come in." Nathan stepped aside. "Sorry, I should've dressed," he stammered. "Is everything okay?" He reached for a shirt that happened to be hanging on the back of the chair to try to ease the awkwardness.

"We need to go to Montrose," Calla Lily said in a rush. "Now," she added as she stepped just inside the doorway.

"Of course. Is something wrong?"

"I got a call from a friend who works at the train station, and he said I need to get there as soon as possible."

"Why? Is someone hurt?" Nathan asked as he buttoned his shirt.

"No, but Lillian arrived and was inquiring where Havenwood Falls is, since it was not clear on her map or from the people she was asking."

"What?" Nathan's eyes went wide. "Give me fifteen minutes, and I can meet you at the shop."

Calla Lily nodded and reached for the door handle. "Sounds good."

"Calla Lily, hi," Amani said with a bright smile.

"Hi to you," she answered. "I'm very sorry I interrupted you both."

"Oh, it's nothing. We were sleeping."

Calla Lily stifled a grin. By the look of Amani's hair and Nathan's bruised lips, sleeping wasn't the only thing that had happened, if it happened at all.

Nathan rubbed the back of his neck and blushed. "A quick cleaning, and I'll be ready to go."

"Where are you going?" Amani asked.

"Calla Lily and I have to go to Montrose. It seems Lillian has decided to come for a visit," Nathan said, hoping to hide the panic in his voice, but Amani could sense his anxiety and looked over at Calla Lily for understanding.

"Everything is fine. We just need to pick her up, and we'll be back after a while," Calla Lily soothed.

Amani reached for Nathan's hands. "Then why are you so nervous?"

"Well, I, uh, haven't exactly told her about you and the secrets here in Havenwood Falls. I'm just not sure how she'll react."

"I'm going to go get the car ready," Calla Lily interjected. "Bye, Amani. I'll see you later."

"See you later. Please be safe on your journey."

"We will," Calla Lily called out just before closing the door.

Amani's face fell. "Will Lillian not like me? Is that why you are so nervous?"

He shook his head. "I don't think that will be the issue. I think she will love you, but now I just have to explain how we met and what you are."

In the moment he said that, two of the pixies Amani had befriended tapped on their window. Amani dragged the sheet behind her and opened the pane. She leaned down and picked them up, bringing them face to face with her. There was a bit of chatter between them, some of which Nathan understood, but he waited until Amani translated before he spoke.

"Hello to you too, Tierri," Nathan responded before he nodded at Ushka. "Where are Enya and Aeiri?" he asked, looking around for the mischievous ones of the bunch.

"Enya set a bush on fire, and Aeiri was fanning the flames," Tierri replied as Ushka simply nodded her head in agreement. "We have to go and help Madame Tahini with them, so we can't stay to work today. Maybe tomorrow we can come back to finish the garden."

Amani and the pixies exchanged blessings and gifts before the two sisters disappeared in a puff of shimmering light.

Nathan sighed. "See, things like this don't happen in New York. We don't have magical fairy gardens and pixies who work with djinns to create a special place for the rabbits to dine."

Amani laughed. "Well, I can explain to Tierri and Ushka that I will return to our work once your guest leaves. And I can promise you I will be on my best behavior. I won't embarrass you."

Nathan pulled her hands to his lips. "You never embarrass me, and Lillian is going to love you."

Amani blushed. "I hope so. I know how much she means to you."

Nathan checked his pocket watch. "I'm sorry. I have to go."

"I will go speak with Mihail and Irina and make sure a room is ready for her when she arrives."

He kissed her once and started to walk away, but went back to kiss her once more. "You're my heart," he said, before he headed off in the direction of Calla Lily's shop.

Nathan didn't know whether to be elated or terrified that Lillian had taken it upon herself to show up in Montrose. How was he going to explain this? Explain Amani? *I know I've intentionally avoided relationships to focus on work, but in the process of finding my father's camera, I've also found the love of my life. Yes, it may be sudden, but there is no one I'd rather spend the rest of my life with. Amani is perfect. Oh no, no, do not worry about her being a thousand or so years old and capable of annihilating cities; she's sweet, loving, and kind.*

"Are you going to continue mumbling or are you ready to go?" Calla Lily asked as she stood by her car.

Nathan laughed nervously. "No. I was just bantering to myself about how to explain Amani, Havenwood Falls, and my need to stay here a bit longer to Lillian. She's rather inquisitive and incredibly persistent."

"You don't have to worry about that. The wards and the Court already make certain the humans remain unaware. Lillian can be in town and not realize there is magic happening all around her, and once she leaves, passing the town's border, she won't remember her time here at all," she said with a grin.

Nathan's brow furrowed as he got into the car. "What do you mean? She won't remember anything?"

"No, she won't."

Nathan rode in silence, sucking in a nervous breath as they drove past the Havenwood Falls sign.

"Don't worry. The wards won't affect you, since you've been approved as a temporary resident," Calla Lily explained.

"For now," he said with an arched brow.

The two passed the rest of the long drive talking about the parchments Lillian had sent a few weeks prior and their connection to Amani and Khalida. They also talked about the glossed-over topic of Calla Lily's lineage. Nathan wanted to know more of what it meant to be a gypsy demon.

"Were you born like that or were you turned into a demon? I mean, can anyone be a supernatural being?"

"No, you cannot be turned, Nathan. I was born a Shuvani. It is similar to a high priestess in any pagan religion."

"I'm completely out of my element here. I've studied the gods of Egypt as a part of my studies, and I've read the old penny dreadfuls my father had packed away in the basement, but other than that, you and Amani are my first magical beings and certainly the only ones who've clued me in to their abilities. I'm still unsure of exactly what Mihail, Irina, and Madame Luiza are." He chuckled. "They're wonderful, but I wouldn't want to get on their bad side for sure."

"They are moroi vampires, and yes, crossing them would be a mistake for sure, but let me try to describe things in terms of what you do know," she said as they made the final curve out of the mountains. "My job as a Shuvani is to ensure the traditions of my kind are passed on to the future generations—for them to understand their abilities."

"What can you do? I mean, can you do things like Amani?"

She cast Nathan a glance. "No one can do what Amani does. At least not that I know of."

Nathan nodded. "Okay then, what are your special talents, beyond being able to see the past like you did with Amani?"

"Now, I can't go and give away all my secrets." She laughed.

"I'm sorry. I didn't mean to pry. My curious nature gets the best of me sometimes."

"I'm teasing you, but we will have to get into this later. We're almost there," Calla Lily said as she turned the Model T onto the main street in Montrose.

"Before we see Lilian, can I ask a favor?"

"Of course," Calla Lily replied.

"Do you have a way to read Lillian without her knowing it?"

"Yes, but may I ask why?"

Nathan ducked his head. "I want to know if she's happy. She's taken care of me ever since my father died, and before that, she filled in as a mother after my real mother died. All Lillian has ever wanted for me was to settle down and have a family of my own." He cast a glance at Calla Lily. "She wants to be a grandmother."

"And now you're worried she'll meet Amani and think she can have all she's ever wanted?"

Nathan nodded.

"But Amani and any children you two could have in the future will be unique, and you'll most likely not be able to be a family the way Lillian envisions."

"It would break her heart, and I can't bear the thought."

"I think we should cross that bridge when we come to it. Right now, we need to focus on the reason she's here to begin with."

As they parked, Nathan scanned the area for any sign of Lillian, while Calla Lily stepped out of the car and made a beeline to meet the man she knew in Montrose. He was the conductor who'd dismissed Nathan when he first arrived and was inquiring about Havenwood Falls. As Nathan watched Calla Lily hug the burly man, he wondered what kind of supernatural he was, if any. He made a note to himself to ask when they were in private as he made his way inside the train station.

There, with a book in one hand and a paper fan in the other, was Lillian with her tattered suitcase sat next to her feet and her black pocketbook tucked in neatly by her side. She must have been engrossed in the story, because she completely missed Nathan standing in front of her.

"I hope you haven't been here too long."

"Oh, Nathan," Lillian cooed as she closed her book and stood to hug him. "It's so good to see you. I've missed you terribly."

"I've missed you too," he said as he returned her embrace. "If I'd known you were coming, I would've been here waiting for you."

"Oh no, no. I wanted to surprise you. When you talked about this place and described how peaceful it was, I just had to see it for myself."

"I'm glad you're here. I'm excited to introduce you to the people I've met. They're wonderful."

"I can't wait." She beamed. "How did you get here?"

"Calla Lily drove me."

"Oh, Calla Lily is it?"

Nathan shook his head. "No. It's not like that. She's just a friend."

Calla Lily walked up behind Nathan and extended her hand in greeting. "You must be Lillian. It's nice to meet you."

The look on Lillian's face spoke volumes as she reluctantly shook Calla Lily's hand, while shoving her book into Nathan's.

"Nathan expected someone older as well." She smiled. "Are these your bags?"

"Yes," Lillian replied, reaching for her suitcase and handbag.

"I've got these, Lillian," Nathan said as he picked up her suitcase. "Good grief. How long do you intend to stay? This thing feels like it's filled with rocks."

"Oh, don't be silly. I packed a few of your things in there as well. You left without your suit and tie. How are you getting along in only your casual clothes?"

Nathan shrugged. "Havenwood Falls isn't like New York, Lillian."

"Well, nonetheless, I brought the navy tweed and your oxfords," she professed, before taking back the book she'd given him.

"What are you reading?" Calla Lily asked as Lillian smoothed the edges on the dust cover.

"This Side of Paradise by F. Scott Fitzgerald. It's a lovely story. Have you read it?"

Calla Lily shook her head.

"Well, you should. I can lend mine to you while I'm here."

"And how long will that be?"

"Nathan Allan Wade, why do you keep asking me that?"

"Just curious is all."

"The car is just out front here," Calla Lily said, hoping to distract them.

CHAPTER 6

*T*he drive back home to Havenwood Falls seemed longer than the last time, but it had more to do with Lillian hammering them both with questions than with the actual distance. She was thoroughly convinced there was something brewing under the surface between Nathan and Calla Lily, and no amount of talking seemed to deflect her inquisition. All of it fell on deaf ears. Lillian had set her sights on the prospect of marriage and children, and there was not going to be anything to deter her—for now at least.

"Lillian, I promise you my relationship with Calla Lily is strictly platonic."

Nathan hoped this declaration would squelch the conversation, because he didn't want to mention Amani until they were all together and he could make the proper introductions.

"Lillian, how was the train ride here? Good, I hope," Calla Lily asked, hoping to change the subject . . . again.

"It was a bit rough at times, but I managed just fine. Thank you for asking." Calla Lily gave Lillian a gentle smile when she turned in her direction. "Colorado is quite a change from New York. This mountain air is heavenly, but being this high up can surely take your breath away."

"Yes, it can, but you'll adjust after a bit. The weather is different than in the city, too, Lillian. It's a different kind of cool—less smoggy." Nathan laughed.

"I can see why you like it here. It beats the heat in Egypt, too," Lillian said as she turned to look back at Nathan in the backseat.

"By far. I love Egypt, but there is something special about Colorado," Nathan replied.

Lillian fell silent as Calla Lily turned onto Main Street and headed toward the inn. She was taking in the town's quaint, inviting features as they slowly made their way over the cobblestone streets. Nathan watched her as she took in the tallest building. It was only three stories and small in comparison to what she was used to seeing. Lillian had been born and raised in New York, and only knew the steel and concrete of the city. She was not used to the tranquility of the country.

"That is quite a charming fountain. We have one in Central Park, but I don't get to enjoy it as often as I'd like," Lillian said as they drove past the town square.

When the car stopped in front of the inn, Nathan got out and opened the door for Lillian, offering his hand to help her out.

"This is lovely," she exclaimed. "What wonderful architecture," she continued as she surveyed the tower and turrets. "I haven't seen one of these since my grandmother Jane moved from Oneida."

"This is where you'll be staying," Nathan said, grabbing her bag and handing her her purse.

"Where I'll be staying? Where will you be?" Lillian inquired. "This is the exact place I made your reservation."

Nathan started to rub the back of his neck, trying to find the words to explain, when Amani walked out the front door of the inn. She took his breath away every time he saw her, but this time was different. She had her hair up in a style befitting the contemporary time period, and she was wearing a dress he could only assume she got from Calla Lily. Amani curtsied at the three of them, quickly moving aside.

Nathan cast a glance at Calla Lily and mouthed, "Was this your doing?"

Calla Lily grinned and walked up next to Lillian. "This way. I will introduce you to Mihail and Irina. They run the inn."

"Oh," she paused, "and is that their daughter?" she asked, tilting her head in Amani's direction as they passed.

"No," Calla Lily stated flatly.

"Madame Luiza has tea waiting for you in the parlor," Amani called out as they stepped onto the porch.

"Thank you, Amani. The dress fits you perfectly, I see," Calla Lily acknowledged.

Amani blushed. "With a little help, yes. Thank you for finding just the right one for me."

When Calla Lily hurried Lillian inside, Nathan made his way to the porch and stopped at the bottom step. "I've never seen you with your hair up. It looks nice."

"I wanted to look like a proper lady of the time and asked Madame Luiza to help me. I was going to use magic, but didn't want to cause any problems while Lillian was here," Amani said as she nervously fiddled with her hair.

Nathan stepped up and stood in front of her. "I don't know what I did to deserve a woman like you, but I do promise to treasure you."

"Oh, Nathan. It is a simple gesture."

"But it's not. It's you doing all you can to fit in to a world where you cannot be who you were made to be," he said as he pulled her close to his chest. "I appreciate it more than I can say." Nathan kissed her softly on the lips. "I'd be happy to show you how much, later, if you'd like," he teased.

"Nathan," Amani scolded, before wrapping her arms around his neck and kissing him again.

Breaking their kiss, Nathan held the door open for Amani, and she began to walk through, but stumbled. "Are you okay?"

"Yes. I just felt a little light-headed all of a sudden. I'll be fine," she said, as she steadied herself with Nathan's help.

"Maybe you should go back to the cottage and rest."

"No. I want to be here. I'd love nothing more than to talk to Lillian once you have introduced me."

Nathan nodded. "On one condition. If you don't feel well while we are visiting, just excuse yourself, and I'll bring you back home."

The smile Amani attempted didn't meet her eyes, but she reluctantly agreed to Nathan's request.

Nathan intertwined their fingers, and the two of them headed toward the parlor.

Laughter filled the room as Irina, Calla Lily, Madame Luiza, and Lillian all chatted and sipped tea. However, the moment the two of them walked into the room, you could have heard a pin drop. Nathan squeezed Amani's hand gently.

"Ladies," he nodded, acknowledging their presence but quickly moving on to address the one person in the room who did not know Amani. Nathan took a deep breath and said, "Lillian, now that you're settled, I'd like you to meet Amani."

The energy in the air seemed to freeze at his announcement. The only sound that could be heard was the nervous shake of Lillian's porcelain cup making contact with its matching saucer. Lillian looked at Calla Lily and then over to Amani beside Nathan.

"Oh. I seem to have . . ." Lillian stammered.

"It's wonderful to meet you, Lillian. I mean Mrs. Hartman," Amani said as she cast an awkward glance at Madame Luiza and Irina, who both smiled with faint nods of encouragement.

Nathan walked, with Amani still by his side, over to the couch where Lillian was sitting. "I didn't say anything on the ride back to town, because I wanted you to meet her in person."

Tears started to well in Lillian's eyes. "And is this young lady the reason you've delayed your return home?"

"Yes, she is," he replied without hesitation.

Lillian stood and pulled Amani into a crushing hug. "I know this is not proper, but I've waited so long for him to find happiness, and now it seems he has."

Relief washed over Nathan as the tension in the room eased, Lillian peppering Amani with questions—some she stammered to answer.

"And are you from here in Colorado, dear?"

"No. I am from . . ."

"She's from Egypt, originally, but has been here in Havenwood Falls for several months," Calla Lily interjected.

Nathan's eyes went wide at the mention of Egypt and the mention of several months, considering it had only been a few weeks. He worried this would be a curiosity Lillian would not skim over—that she would instead home in on the connection—but was pleasantly surprised when Lillian exclaimed, "Egypt! No wonder Nathan was fascinated by you. Between your beauty and his love of all things Egyptian, this was destined."

The five women and Nathan visited in the parlor for a bit, until it was time for Madame Luiza to begin cooking dinner for the inn's guests. She told them that she'd made a pot roast with all the trimmings for Lillian's first meal with them. She thought it was only fitting to welcome her the same way she welcomed Nathan.

"You must try the biscuits with her blueberry jam. They're amazing." Amani beamed.

"Amani had never had blueberry jam before she came to Havenwood Falls. I'm sure if she had some elsewhere, she'd love theirs, too," Madame Luiza interjected.

"It sounds delicious. I make a cinnamon-spiced pear jam. We should exchange recipes," Lillian replied.

The bell rang at the front desk, and Irina rose from the couch. "Please excuse me. It's been a busy day of check-ins, and Mihail needs help escorting someone up to their room. I will find you when I'm finished."

"Anything I can help with?" Amani offered.

"No, you enjoy the company. I will come find you if we can't manage it," Irina answered.

Nathan pulled out chairs for Amani and then Lillian, before he moved to do the same for Calla Lily. It was just in time too, since Madame Luiza was bringing plates in to tempt their senses.

"Everything looks delicious, Madame Luiza. Thank you," Nathan said as he took a seat next to Amani.

"I hope you all enjoy. I'll check on you in a bit," Madame Luiza said, excusing herself to head back toward the kitchen.

As Madame Luiza left the room, Lillian looked at Calla Lilly and Amani. "I swear I must be the oldest person here. Everyone I've met so far is young. I look like a dowager compared to all of you."

Nathan started to fidget, but Calla Lily replied to settle his nerves. "We do have older residents. You just haven't had the pleasure of meeting them yet."

"Oh. Have you lived here in Havenwood Falls long, Calla Lily?" Lillian asked.

"I've been here a few years."

"And are you married? Children?"

"Lillian," Nathan scolded.

"I'm just curious. A beautiful young woman like yourself should've been scooped up by now."

Amani sat quietly, unsure of what to say. She wasn't familiar with this type of conversation. She almost felt embarrassed that she'd never thought to ask Calla Lily if she had someone special in her life. Amani cast a sorrowful glance at Calla Lily before looking at Nathan, who was visibly agitated by Lillian's line of questioning. The hair on Lillian's head started to float, as if she'd just been doused by a surge of electricity. Calla Lily and Nathan tried to remain composed, hoping Lillian didn't notice. Amani, however, was wringing her hands.

"What's wrong, dear?" Lillian asked.

"Nothing," Amani said with a quick shake of her head. "I . . . I . . ." Amani stood and rushed away from the table.

Calla Lily stood a moment later. "I'll go check on her." Nathan nodded, and she eased him with the touch of her hand on his. "There is nothing to worry about. I'm sure it's just nerves."

"Did I say something wrong?" Lillian questioned.

"No, but you may need to lessen the inquisition, Lillian. We're not in New York, and these people are less like the gossip circle of ladies you meet with on Thursdays," he said with a faint smile.

Lillian dipped her chin. "Of course. I meant no harm."

"I know, but I would appreciate it if you wouldn't put your nose in Calla Lily's business."

"She's lovely, you know," she said as she unfolded her napkin and placed it in her lap.

"Amani or Calla Lily?"

"Both, but I specifically meant Amani."

"Yes, she is," he said as he too placed his napkin in his lap. "If I am being honest, I can say without a doubt that I've fallen in love with her."

Lillian smiled a broad, proud smile. "Well, it is about time."

"I knew you were going to say that."

"Are you going to ask her to marry you?"

"I haven't gotten that far yet. The only thing I know is that I only ever want her."

"It is sudden, but I know well enough that when you know, you know. That is how I fell in love with Charles. Two hours at the garden party my aunt Edith had, and I was ready to go that evening to the minister and start our new life."

Nathan leaned forward. "And did you?"

"No, he needed to get my father's blessing first and then we had to wait for a few months after that for his parents to return from a family trip, but the moment everyone was back, we went the very next day." Lillian inhaled. "I loved him every day since that first moment."

"I don't think you've ever shared this story with me."

She patted his hand. "Never had the occasion, it seems, until now."

Madame Luiza arrived at the table with a tray of desserts, placing two of them in front of Nathan and Lillian.

"Where are Calla Lily and Amani?" Madame Luiza asked.

"They should be right back. I don't think Amani was feeling too well and excused herself," Nathan replied, his eyes speaking the words he could not in front of Lillian.

Madame Luiza got the message and patted Nathan on the shoulder. "I'll go check on them, but in the meantime, you two go ahead and enjoy the cobbler. I used fresh blueberries from the garden."

"Thank you, Madame Luiza."

When she left, Lillian took a bite of the cobbler and moaned. "These have to be the best blueberries I have ever put in my mouth. They're almost magical."

Nathan laughed nervously. "Yep, magical indeed."

CHAPTER 7

"*A*mani, are you okay?" Calla Lily asked when she found her in the corner down the hall.

"No. Something's wrong."

"What?" Calla Lily asked in a panic.

Amani turned her hands over and tried to hold them steady for Calla Lily to see. Gold hieroglyphs shimmered on the surface of her skin, while trails of silver flowed through them, creating sparks of energy that popped and shimmered. Calla Lily reached out to touch her, but Amani reeled back. "I don't want to hurt you."

Madame Luiza came around the corner and rushed to Calla Lily's side. "What's wrong? What can we do, Amani?"

Amani had slid down the wall and was curled into a ball, trying to contain the energy surging through her. She was pleading with herself to calm down. The problem was, she wasn't upset and couldn't for the life of her understand why this was happening.

"Help me. I don't want to change. I cannot allow my djinn to surface," Amani cried.

"I can help, Amani. I promise," Calla Lily soothed.

"Do you remember the tea you made with the lavender and valerian root?" Calla Lily asked Madame Luiza.

"Of course."

"Can you please add some passion flower and some lemon balm? I think that, with a bit of magic, will calm and soothe our girl," Calla Lily said in a calm clear voice.

Madame Luiza didn't hesitate. Instead she moved in a blur to do as Calla Lily asked. When she returned, Amani was sobbing and was paler than normal.

"Do you trust me?" Calla Lily asked as she took the mug from Madame Luiza.

"Of course," Amani replied, looking into Calla Lily's eyes. "I'll do anything to stop this."

"Good." Calla Lily inhaled slowly before chanting words Amani and Madame Luiza were unfamiliar with. As she continued to spell the tea with her gypsy magic, it began to boil and smoke before settling. When Calla Lily handed the mug to Amani, it was cold to the touch.

"Drink it all. It will make you sleepy, but don't worry. We'll take care of you and get you back to the cottage, okay?"

Amani nodded and drank the tea without hesitation. The gold and silver threads receded, and Amani's eyes grew heavy. Calla Lily moved next to her and steadied Amani, holding her in her arms until she was asleep.

"That was close," Calla Lily sighed.

"What was that? The stress of Lillian being here?" Madame Luiza asked.

"No, it came on suddenly, and there was true panic in her face as it was happening. Hopefully when she wakes, we can ask her more questions."

"Do you want me to go get Nathan?"

"No, I don't want to alert Lillian to it, and he won't be able to hide his emotion over something being wrong with Amani. Let's just get her back to the cottage."

With vampire strength, Madame Luiza carried Amani to the cottage and settled her on the couch while Calla Lily started a fire.

"Can you please let Nathan know, after Lillian is in her room, that I'm here with Amani and will stay until he can be with her?" Calla Lily asked.

"Of course. Are you sure you'll be okay?" Madame Luiza responded.

Calla Lily gave a faint smile. "That concoction will knock her out for at least nine hours, if not more."

"You're certain?" Madame Luiza insisted.

"One hundred percent. That spell has never failed me, supernatural or not."

"I'll bring you a plate in a few so you can eat while you wait."

"Thank you, Madame Luiza."

She gave a clipped nod and closed the door behind her.

"I don't know what happened tonight, Amani, but we'll find out. I promise," Calla Lily said as she laid a quilt over Amani's sleeping form.

Calla Lily wasn't sure how much time had passed, but it was enough that Madame Luiza had come and gone with dinner and long enough for her to tidy up the cottage to pass the time.

When Nathan walked in the door, he was concerned but not shaken. However, the moment he saw Amani lying motionless and Calla Lily holding her hand while she slept, he became alarmed. "What's wrong? Madame Luiza said she wanted to rest and that she sent her apologies. I didn't think anything was wrong other than that. If I'd have known—"

"There wouldn't have been anything for you do to anyway. You were better suited entertaining Lillian."

Nathan tugged off his jacket and laid it over the back of the chair. "Tell me what happened."

"She started to lose control. Energy started to surge through her, and she was afraid of her djinn side surfacing."

"Why? Was it all the questions Lillian was asking?"

"No, I think it's something else, or shall I say someone else."

"Who? Is Roman doing this?" Nathan snapped.

Calla Lily shook her head. "No. Actually, I think it's Khalida, but I cannot be certain. I've been trying to read her thoughts while she sleeps, but I can only get flashes of images. Nothing that makes any sense, but when Amani's hieroglyphs were surfacing, silver trails flowed through them, which as you know is indicative of Khalida's power, not Amani's."

Nathan sat in the chair opposite Calla Lily. "I didn't think Khalida could be a problem anymore. I guess I thought wrong."

"Maybe Amani will know more when she wakes, but that won't be until tomorrow sometime. I spelled her tea." Nathan's eyes went wide, causing Calla Lily to quickly add, "She knew and wanted me to do anything to stop the change. She'll be fine."

Nathan nodded. "You look exhausted. You should head home."

"I am tired," Calla Lily said as she stood. "I'll be by in the morning to check on her."

"I'm sorry I can't walk you home," Nathan said as they made their way to the door.

Calla Lily stifled her laugh. "I appreciate the sentiment, Nathan, but I can more than take care of myself."

Nathan chuckled in response. "Yeah, I assume so. See you in the morning then."

"Unless something with her changes, then send for me right away, okay?"

"Hopefully she'll get some rest and be better in the morning."

Calla Lily touched Nathan's forearm. "We'll figure this out," she said as she turned to leave. "And Nathan, make sure she knows you're near. You soothe her, and she needs that."

Nathan's lips turned upward. "I will. Thank you again."

"You're welcome," she replied as she walked onto the path next to the garden. "Goodnight, Nathan."

"Goodnight, Calla Lily."

CHAPTER 8

*N*athan lifted Amani off the couch and carried her to the bed, where he could keep close watch over her. She slept through the night, but it was a fitful sleep. Amani cried out in pain several times when silver and gold hieroglyphs appeared and disappeared on her skin. Nathan tried to make them out, but they were gone before he could recognize any of them. When her hair started to change from blond to black, he really became worried. She didn't look well. She was pale and clammy to the touch, and even though her eyes were still closed, it appeared as though Amani was struggling against something or someone. When the morning light started to peek into the windows, Nathan went into the bathroom to splash some water on his face.

Nathan heard a knock on the door. Softly at first, but then again, a little more aggressively.

"Nathan? Amani? It's Calla Lily," he heard her call out from the other room. Nathan made his way to the door and opened it.

"You look awful," Calla Lily professed.

"Thanks. That's what no sleep gets you."

"Did she not sleep through the night?"

"She did and she didn't. She never once woke, but things were happening unbeknownst to her. I don't know," Nathan said, running his fingers through his already tousled hair.

"Is she still sleeping?"

He nodded.

"Go get cleaned up, and I will stay with her. I can't imagine she'll be asleep much longer."

"All right," Nathan relented, "I'll be quick."

"THOTH?" Amani questioned. "Am I dreaming?"

"Not exactly, child. You are still entranced, thanks to your friend, who I must say, is quite the skilled alchemist. But I've bypassed it to speak to you directly."

"I'm certain she will appreciate the compliment," Amani said as she sat up and stared up at Thoth. "How is this possible for me to be up and around and yet still out from her elixir?"

"I woke your subconscious. I need your help, and I didn't want to do anything without your consent."

Amani's brows furrowed. "Is Khalida consenting?"

"No. She's fighting me every step of the way."

Amani nodded. "What do you need from me?"

"Some of your blood and answers."

Amani extended both of her arms, wrists up, toward Thoth. "Whatever you need."

Thoth took her wrist in his hand and began to call forth her blood. It rose up like it had with Khalida and floated in a stream from her to the vial he was holding. Vibrant gold flecks with hints of copper shone as if lit by an unseen light.

"Interesting," he said aloud.

"Is something wrong?"

"I've never seen cooper in your blood, Amani. May I?" he asked as he closed the vial and began to move his hand to her forehead.

She replied by leaning in, her head slightly bowed in his direction.

Thoth's touch was gentle as he read her thoughts and her internal systems. The answer he was looking for was right there.

"You mated with Nathan?"

"Yes," Amani whispered, a blush pinking her cheeks.

"This explains a lot, but also offers an additional challenge."

"Why is that?" she asked as she stared up at him, her eyes pleading.

"Because, my dear one, you are with child."

Amani's face fell. "What?"

"You are well within the age of maturity for reproduction. It is the way of the djinn, and while it is preferred you mate with your own kind, as you know, you are unique, and therefore there is no one else like you."

The information swirled in Amani's brain as she asked, "But what about Khalida? I'm connected to her, but will she now be connected to my child?"

"I have a bit more work to do, and now with your blood, I may be even closer. I need one answer, though, before I can proceed." Amani nodded. "How many times have you sensed Khalida? Felt her as if you were connected?"

"I've always felt her. The first time you put us in the temple jars, I had to find ways to block her rage, to protect myself from it."

"And can she sense you the same way?"

"Yes, but I'm not sure if it's exactly the same."

"And why is that?"

"She always keeps a part of herself hidden. I think it's too dark even for her to embrace, until she wants to. I've felt her anger more and more since I killed Khaldun."

"I see," he said curiously, "and the blocking you are doing isn't helping?"

"It only lessens the intensity. Nothing more."

"Very good. I think I know what is happening and how this came to be," he affirmed. "I need a bit more time, and then we may proceed. In the meantime, I think you may need to inform Nathan that his life is about to change even further."

"Is everything going to be all right? Please be honest with me. I've never had anything to lose once my parents died, but now with Nathan and—" she looked down at her belly—"a baby to consider, I don't want to hope for too much and end up heartbroken."

"I still have a few things to sort, but after your answers here, I can say that one piece of the puzzle has been solved. You and Khalida are not twins, as originally thought, but instead, one and the same. Rather, you're the same person split in two. It explains everything."

"What?" Terror flashed over her features. "That can't be."

"Everyone has light and dark within them, and in your case, you and Khalida were split the moment of your creation. The details are what I need to work out, and I will. In the meantime, you should only concern yourself with Nathan and the child. Understand?"

"I'm scared. What if he is angry about becoming a father so soon? And what kind of mother will I be, knowing I am not a whole person and could lose control at any time?"

"That is an unlikely outcome on both fronts. I doubt he will feel anything other than elation at the thought. In regards to you losing control—" he shook his head and a grin tipped his lips—"you're a djinn whether you've been split or not. Anything could trigger the parts of you that are not human-like. This façade before me is not the whole of you. You are special. Stop hiding that and embrace the gifts it brings you."

"Thank you, Thoth, for all you've done for me."

"You are welcome, but it is I who should be thanking you. You had the answers to the riddle." Thoth tilted his head at Amani and disappeared via wisps of sand.

When Thoth left, Amani lay back and rejoined her body, lying peacefully for a few moments before sitting up in bed and laying her hand on her belly.

CHAPTER 9

*K*halida woke the moment Thoth returned. She tried to act as though she were still asleep, but Thoth knew otherwise.

"Your games may work on others, but they are lost on me," he said as he put the vial of Amani's shimmering blood next to the one he'd taken from Khalida earlier.

"I'm not playing games. I'm not interested in being used as an experiment."

"I will need another bit of your blood to test a theory."

"You're actually asking this time?"

"I'll ask only once."

Khalida's eyes flashed a mixture of gold and blue, and went from clear to opaque as hieroglyphs erupted on her neck and arms.

"What have you done to me?" she cried out as she put her hand on her stomach.

"Nothing, but it seems your connection to Amani is just as I thought."

"What does that mean?" she snarled.

"It means you feel what she feels and vice versa."

Khalida stood and glared at Thoth. "Then why am I the one in here, and she is the one free to roam the earth?"

"Not the earth, just the small town you and Khaldun tried to conquer. Does that answer your question?"

"Let me out of here!" Khalida raged, slamming her fists against the invisible barrier.

"Do you know any other forms of communication besides rage and deception? I've grown tired of your childish tantrums."

Khalida transformed, releasing the djinn just below the surface. Inside her cage, she arced electrical currents from her fingertips, loving it when they bounced off the barrier and surged back into her. Her now white hair blustered, while silver-blue streaks danced over her skin. "If you will not release me, I will make it my mission to torture your pet."

Thoth crossed his arms in front of his chest and let her play her game. Until he heard Amani's pleas. Thoth turned to see where they were coming from when the blood in the vial began to swirl in a vortex, shattering the glass. The blood hovered midair and howled as Khalida continued to wreak havoc.

"STOP, KHALIDA! ENOUGH!" Amani's voice boomed in an echo inside the invisible prison, their connection stronger than ever.

When Khalida laughed, the blood above Thoth's head rushed to break the barrier of the cage, but when the attempt failed, the crimson liquid burst into flames. Thoth watched in amazement the power the two wielded. However, since Khalida was the only one contained, he snapped his fingers, silencing the two djinn. Khalida fell to the floor with a thud, and Thoth hoped Amani was somewhere where she hadn't hurt anyone, or herself.

"The merging must take place sooner rather than later, but I will not be able to do it alone," he said as he disappeared into thin air.

"NATHAN!" Calla Lily screamed from the bedroom.

Nathan tore back to Amani's side, only to find her hovering above the bed, her skin dusky grey and her hair ablaze.

"Amani, what's wrong? What's happening?" he pleaded.

"She can't hear us, Nathan. Khalida is doing something to her," Calla Lily said as they watched Amani talk to someone not seen or heard.

"What do we do?" Nathan pleaded.

Calla Lily began to chant. At first, nothing happened, but she continued as the air around them became dense.

"What is this? What are you doing?"

"Blocking her energy as best I can. The last thing we need is for Roman and the Court to show up and see her like this."

Calla Lily had yet to finish her chant when Amani screamed, "STOP, KHALIDA! ENOUGH!"

Amani's arms flew wide, her full djinn on display as white-hot energy blasted from her, knocking Nathan and Calla Lily to the floor. She collapsed back onto the bed, and within moments, changed back into her human self, passing out as she did. As the last bit of Amani's skin returned to its natural color, Roman, Mihail, Irina, Madame Luiza, Ric Kasun, Saundra Beaumont, Tierri, and Ushka all burst into the cottage.

"Everything is okay," Calla Lily announced, holding up her hands to stop the onslaught of questions as she and Nathan stood to regain their footing.

"Do you have any idea how much energy just surged through the town?" Roman snarled.

"Yes, Roman. I have an idea, since I watched it all happen from only a few feet away," Calla Lily remarked.

Roman glared at her, but it was Ric who spoke next. "What happened?"

Calla Lily looked to Amani, who was still unconscious, but now wrapped in Nathan's arms. "Honestly, we don't know. She was asleep and then all of a sudden her djinn side emerged and she started to scream at Khalida."

"Khalida was here?" Saundra exclaimed.

"No," Nathan replied, "she was talking to the air."

Madame Luiza, Tierri, and Ushka made their way past Roman and Ric and went over to Amani. Beads of sweat lay untouched on her forehead, and her breathing was labored. Tierri appeared to flit about, landing on the bed near Amani's shoulder. The pixies took one look at Amani and knew what to do. Ushka disappeared and reappeared in a flash with a pail of water and two African violet plants. She and Tierri hurriedly lay the petals over Amani's neck and used the water to cool her skin. Tierri whispered something to Madame Luiza, who then repeated the sentiment to the crowd. "The water from the falls and violets will work to soothe her."

"The danger has passed, but she shouldn't be agitated," Calla Lily added.

"Well, I don't want to be agitated either, and yet I am," Roman balked. "Why do you all continue to protect a woman capable of destroying this town? Why is she worth such loyalty?"

Tierri and Ushka gasped and were suddenly in Roman's face, scolding him for saying something so vicious. Ric tried to calm the pixies, but he was getting a kick out of the tongue-lashing they were giving Roman. Tierri was going on and on about how he was insufferable and inconsiderate of someone who has done nothing but be gracious and kind.

"Amani's my friend. And that I'll defend!" Tierri declared.

"Me too!" Ushka added.

Both pixies looked around, waiting for the "me three" and "me four" they were accustomed to hearing from their sisters.

Roman didn't reply, but the snarl on his face spoke volumes.

Ric clapped Roman on the shoulder. "It seems we should all get going. Tierri, Ushka, Calla Lily, and Nathan seem more than capable of taking care of Amani," he said before nodding at Madame Luiza, who was still sitting next to Amani. "I hope Amani feels better soon. If you need me for anything, let me know."

"Thank you, Ric." Madame Luiza nodded.

Everyone moved to leave, but Roman stood his ground.

"There is nothing left for us to uncover, Roman," Mihail said sternly. "I think it's time to leave. Now," he insisted.

Roman sneered and started to speak, but Saundra nudged him forward, and he finally made his way out the door of the cottage.

Saundra turned back before she walked out. "If she needs anything, Calla Lily, I'm happy to help. She doesn't look well."

"Thank you, Saundra."

"I'll bring some tea and towels back in few," Irina added as she waited for Mihail.

"I'll check in later as well," Mihail said, before pulling the door closed.

Tierri and Ushka continued to fuss over Amani, as Madame Luiza touched her forehead. "I think she has a fever, but then other times she feels cold as ice. What should we do?"

Calla Lily shrugged and turned to Nathan.

"I feel helpless," he answered.

"There's no need," a voice said behind them. They spun around, their mouths agape as they stared at Thoth. "I've got what she needs."

Calla Lily and Nathan stepped aside as Madame Luiza stood. Tierri and Ushka sailed to where Nathan was standing, resting on his shoulders, watching as the god made his way to Amani's side.

"I was here earlier, talking to her."

"What?" Calla Lily exclaimed. "When? She's been asleep this entire time."

"Yes, she has. You made an effective elixir, I might add."

"Thank you, but that doesn't answer the question." She crossed her arms.

"I was speaking to her through her subconscious. Not long before she lost control and released her djinn."

"How did you know?" Nathan interjected.

"Because Khalida intentionally set hers free and was agitating Amani to do the same. The blood she gave me earlier reacted and burst into flames. I knew then what was happening."

"The blood she gave you? When did Amani give you her blood?" Nathan asked.

"I was here earlier checking on her."

"Then what is wrong with her now? Why isn't she awake?" Madame Luiza added.

"I had to put them both in a trance, but between my power and the Shuvani's elixir, it seems to have had an adverse reaction."

"Oh dear, I never meant to . . ." Calla Lily stammered.

"You did nothing wrong," Thoth interrupted. "This was all Khalida's doing." He touched Amani's head and snapped his fingers, and Amani's eyes opened. "There you are, sweet one."

Amani's voice shook. "Please tell me I didn't hurt anyone. I didn't mean to lose control."

"I'm afraid that was Khalida's doing, but it was all worth it."

"Worth it?" Nathan exclaimed, forgetting for a moment whom he was yelling at.

Thoth nodded. "Yes, because now I know how to fix it."

"Really?" Amani questioned.

"They are not twins, as we all previously thought."

"Then what are they?" Calla Lily asked.

"They are one and the same. Two halves of a whole . . . light and dark split. It is my belief that when Sekhmet and Shu used their powers to attack one another, a different kind of being, not previously seen, was created. They were djinn, as others of their kind are because they are made of fiery wind. However, when Sekhmet and Shu continued to argue, the *whole* was split in two. It explains why they have elements of both, and yet those elements are housed in different beings. Amani is the empathetic one, while Khalida carries all the rage," Thoth finished.

"But . . ." Nathan muttered.

"If one dies, so will the other—that is true," Thoth continued. "Therefore, we must merge the two halves and make them whole again."

"What if I'm not strong enough? What if she takes over?" Amani said, her chin trembling. "I don't want to die."

"This is insane. Make them whole or she'll die or Khalida will die," Nathan stammered over his thoughts. "How can you even think about doing something like this?" he said, running his hands through his hair before reaching for Amani's hand.

"It will not be easy, but it can be done. They are the same person.

When one is balanced by the other, they will no longer need to fight for dominance."

"But through all of this, how can we be certain which half will emerge as the dominant personality?" Nathan asked, his voice unsteady.

Thoth turned to face him. "Amani. She is the stronger of the two. Khalida was only strong when Amani wasn't around to combat her. With the two of them connected, they feed off one another. Khalida is trying to use that to tip Amani over the edge and prove she is the dominant one, but I know the truth."

"And what will this mean in the end?" Calla Lily asked. "If they are *merged* as you say, where will that leave Amani?"

"She will be the djinn she was intended to be. The Amani we know will remain, but she will also have traits of Khalida. One will balance the other."

"I'm going to be like Khalida?" Amani said shakily. "I don't want to be anything like her. And what about . . ."

"Everything will be fine. You are stronger than you think you are. You always have been, and that is even without her influence. Soon you'll be a force to be reckoned with."

"Heavens, isn't she that now?" Madame Luiza joked, hoping to ease the tension in the room.

Everyone went silent, but when Tierri and Ushka giggled, the rest of them joined in.

CHAPTER 10

hankful for the break in tension, Tierri and Ushka went about helping to clean up a bit. Tierri ordered Ushka to fetch some more water from the falls and bring it back posthaste, to help with the color in Amani's cheeks.

"She still looks flushed. The water will bring her back to good health," Tierri insisted.

When Ushka returned, Thoth was intrigued, as the water seemed to glisten the moment it touched Amani's skin.

"What is this? It's like no water I've ever seen . . ."

"It falls from the falls! The Great Falls falls," Ushka replied.

"May I?" Thoth asked, extending his hand.

"It's magic!" Ushka said, handing him a small bucket filled with the shimmering liquid.

Tierri piped in, "She means it's imbued with magic."

"Magic?" Thoth questioned, pouring a bit of it in his hand and dipping his fingers into it. "Interesting composition. How did it come to be filled with this 'magic'?"

"According to Ric and Gaby Kasun, centuries ago, a witch and her family were here in our canyon, and she left a gift for all of us," Madame Luiza answered.

"It's quite the gift," Thoth replied. "Do you know what gives it the special qualities?"

"Aether," she stated flatly. "We were blessed to have been given it, and it has been cherished. Why do you find it so intriguing, though?"

"Because I think it may hold the key to the merging. This, combined with the goddesses' magic and mine—" Thoth paused to look over at Calla Lily—"and your gifts, will keep Amani safe and the merge a success."

"You want my help?" Calla Lily questioned.

"You have the skill, and you are close to Amani. The combination will be welcome, if not necessary to ground her. Will you assist?"

"Absolutely. Without question."

"Very good," Thoth said as he stood. "Do you mind if I take some of this liquid aether? I want to do some tests to confirm my hypothesis."

"That is not much. Would you like me to take to you to the source?" Calla Lily offered.

Thoth nodded. "Yes, more would be helpful and would give us a chance to speak further."

"Very well," Calla Lily said, moving toward the door. "It's about a fifteen-minute walk."

Thoth moved toward her and held out his hand. "Care to travel another way?" he said with a tilted grin.

Calla Lily was taken aback at first, but then put her hand in his, an electrical charge surging through the two of them. In the blink of an eye, the two were gone in a vortex of sand.

"I don't know how it's possible that there is never a speck of sand left when he or Amani disappears," Madame Luiza said with a shake of her head.

⤳

THOTH AND CALLA LILY arrived near the waterfall, and Calla Lily took a moment to catch her breath.

"Wow, that is certainly a way to travel," she said as her hand lingered in Thoth's. The images flashing in her brain were rapid and vivid. Thoth stood before her in his ceremonial garb, decked out as any god of his stature, but the god she was seeing with her sight was far different—more relaxed.

Thoth grinned at the blush in Calla Lily's cheeks. "I apologize. I didn't mean to fluster you."

"I'm not flustered. I simply wasn't expecting to see so much of you in those visions."

"I'm not usually impressed by the skill set of ordinary witches, but then again, you are no ordinary anything, are you, Calla Lily?"

"No. Ordinary would not be a term used to describe me," she said as she continued to meet his gaze.

"I'd assume not."

Calla Lily cleared her throat and turned toward the water. "It's exquisite, isn't it? There is something soothing about the peacefulness of the water after it makes its trek down the thunderous fall," she said, walking to the water's edge and dipping her hand into the pond.

"Where is the aether? It looks like an ordinary body of water," Thoth asked.

"Right here," she answered, pulling up a handful of the shimmering, glittery liquid.

"It hides itself until it is touched?"

"Everything here in Havenwood Falls is not what it seems. I like to think of it as self-preservation." Calla Lily winked.

"This place is unique, I will admit that, but why the secrecy?"

"We are all special and have many qualities the human world would be frightened of. Their fear leads to their aptitude for violence. We merely want to live in peace. Here we can do that."

"And yet you have some among you who lack tolerance?"

"Roman can be difficult, but he does it to keep us all safe. Rules are in place for that to remain possible."

"Why does he feel Amani poses a risk to him?" He paused. "Yes, her djinn side can be intimidating, but the things that occurred when she first arrived were her attempt to protect. She never intended to harm innocents. Amani is not the one out to destroy."

"No, she's not, and most of us know that, but Roman sees things differently than most."

"This Roman only sees things in his own favor."

Calla Lily chuckled. "Well, I cannot argue with that."

"I have not spoken with Hathor and Ma'at, but I know they will agree once I explain my position."

Calla Lily's brows ticked upward. "Your position on what?"

"I feel the need to perform the merging here in Havenwood Falls, right here near the aether. Its power and energy will sustain Amani in the event Khalida tries to take over."

"I thought you said Amani would emerge the victor."

"And she will, but I'm afraid there is always a chance Khalida could weaken Amani to try to gain the advantage."

"What do we do if that happens? None of us will stand for losing Amani—especially not Nathan." Calla Lily sighed. "And he's hardly capable of protecting her, since he's human."

"All precautions and actions will be taken to make certain that does not happen."

"And what do we about Nathan and the Court? How are we to include them in this process?"

"Like you, Nathan is a necessity for Amani's sake. Your friend Roman and the rest of the 'court' as you call them, should be aware of the plan, but they must not interfere."

Calla Lily scoffed. "You're asking for quite a lot if you think Roman will agree to that. I am certain the others will come around, but him?" She blew out a breath. "I'll see what I can do to convince them."

"I'm hoping to wait until the new moon on the twelfth of September. I think with everything else planned, it yields the most favorable time to perform the merging. Do you agree?"

"You're asking my opinion?"

"Why not?" Thoth asked as he made her personal tarot deck appear in her hands. "I know Amani showed you the way with those when she first arrived. Care to try again?"

Calla Lily stared up at him in confusion. "How did you know

that?"

"I know everything."

"Humble, I see."

"I mean simply that I'm aware." Thoth tilted his head in the direction of her hands. "If you look, you'll see what I mean."

Calla Lily knelt down and began to run her hands over the cards, connecting her energy to them. "What am I supposed to be looking for?"

"Nothing more than the evidence of what I believe will be our success."

She closed her eyes and used her Shuvani gifts, whispering enchantments and incantations before pulling the first card. "The High Priestess," she whispered. "The archetype within. The representation of us that descends to hell and back, but not without bestowing symbolic lessons to coincide with it."

"What else do you see?"

"11:11 gateway? The High Priestess is between the light and dark pillars." Calla Lily questioned, "It can't be?"

Thoth gave her an apathetic look, kneeling down beside her. "And yet it is. Khalida and Amani are represented here and here." He pointed. "With Hathor's depiction at the center of it all."

"That is not Hathor," she protested.

"Not exactly, but the horned diadem does represent her in a way, does it not?"

"I . . . I don't know what to say."

"Say you will speak to your Court and show them the proof of my hypothesis. The blue in the High Priestess's robes is a symbol of water, and all of the pieces of the puzzle come together and culminate to one place."

"Havenwood Falls," she answered.

"Yes, on the twelfth, here by the aether and while the new moon is overhead."

"It's not a lot of time to prepare. That is only a few days away."

"At the rate Khalida is surging, it could be several days of torment for Amani. I will do my best to control the phasing between them, but in the meantime, you need to make sure the Court is ready when we return."

Calla Lily nodded, but remained stoic until Thoth reached for her free hand and brought it to his lips.

"I know it's a lot to take in, but you are powerful, and I trust that your power of persuasion will turn this situation in our favor."

More images fluttered in her mind, and the corners of her mouth curved into a smile as she studied him. "I never imagined a god flirting to get what he wants."

"I'm not flirting to get what I want. I always get what I want. I'm simply showing you potential options."

"Oh," she said softly, a grin forming as she continued to watch the images playing in her vision.

"There is one more card amidst the deck that you need to take heed of," he said as he touched the deck in her left hand. "It will enlighten a thought you've yet to think of."

"All right?"

"Until we meet again, Calla Lily Mircea," Thoth said before vanishing into a vortex of sand.

"No ride home?" She sighed.

Calla Lily began to make her way back to the road by way of the forest path, but was stopped when the sound of twigs snapping caught her attention.

"That was quite the exit."

"Excuse me?" she demanded as Roman moved out of the shadows and into view. "Were you spying on us?"

"Didn't seem like much to spy on, but I do find the consistent presence of him annoying."

"Twice doesn't make it consistent," she huffed, walking past him.

"Why was he here again, and why were you both here by the aether?"

"If it wasn't so late and I wasn't so tired, I'd stop to explain, but you are just going to have to wait until I am good and ready to tell you. Until then, try a little patience, Roman. It might do you some good."

"I wonder if you have overextended your welcome here in Havenwood Falls, Miss Mircea," Roman shouted as she continued to walk on, putting some distance between them.

She stopped and turned back. "No, but do try your best to remove me. It might be fun to watch you fail," Calla Lily responded, her voice echoing.

Calla Lily gripped the cards in her hand, ignoring the rest of the ignorant, arrogant remarks Roman continued to call out. Thankful to finally be out of earshot of him, she could see the Whisper Falls Inn sign and was relieved to almost be back to the cottage. Roman's idle threat meant nothing, but it would make it harder to present Thoth's plan to the Court if he was going to constantly be interrupting with his venomous words.

Calla Lily made her way onto the path, but tripped on a loose rock. The cards in her hand flew into the air and landed in a scattered mess on the moss. All of the cards but one landed face down. The one card that shone in the moonlight was the Empress in all her glory, the bright yellow background a beacon declaring the card's meaning. The Empress sat on her throne, wearing a starry crown and holding a scepter in her right hand. *Stability, abundance, nurturing, and new opportunities.* Calla Lilly gathered all the cards, taking one last look at the Empress before flipping it over and pocketing the tarot deck in her skirt.

"Message received, Thoth," she whispered, turning the handle on the cottage door. "I'm back," Calla Lily announced.

CHAPTER 11

"*J*thought you were only going to grab some of the aether. What took so long?" Madame Luiza asked. "Are you all right?"

Calla Lily nodded. "Yes, I'm fine. It took a little extra time. Thoth was explaining the plan for what's to come and the things we need to do."

"Nothing to be worried about, I hope?"

"I'll explain later," Calla Lily said in a low tone. "How's Amani?"

"Much better. She's resting. Nathan is in there with her now, and Tierri and Ushka said they'd return tomorrow with more violets and some poppy milk, just in case you need to make a stronger potion for Amani."

"They are too kind."

"Hey. Glad you're back. How was your visit with the God of Wisdom?" Nathan teased, as he walked out of the bedroom.

"I'd assume like any other conversation you'd have with a god."

Nathan laughed. "Human here. My chats with God are more like, 'bless this food' or 'can you heal the sick.' The stuff going on here is a bit epic. It's a lot to digest."

Calla Lily grinned. "And yet, you're doing a great job of it."

Nathan rubbed his forehead. "Do you two have any thoughts on what I should do with Lillian? Do I pretend like none of this is going on? Send her home early? I mean, you said it yourself—she won't remember any of this once she leaves."

"There is no denying her timing couldn't have been worse, but now that she's here and has seen you and met Amani, do you think she'll go back without a word?" Calla Lily asked.

Nathan shook his head. "Not likely. Not until she can spend some more time getting to know Amani."

"Well, then I say we take it day by day. I could make an elixir to wipe her thoughts daily, but I'm not sure that will be helpful," Calla Lily said with a shrug.

"I say you don't do a thing. Let her see and experience whatever she will experience and it won't matter. The wards will keep the magic of it all hidden from her sight, and the memories will be wiped anyway once she leaves. She could see Amani go full djinn, but she'll never take that back to New York," Madame Luiza added.

"That is true," Calla Lily interjected. "We'll just need to keep her safe. Beyond that, it will all go away."

Nathan frowned. "She'll never even remember meeting her here, will she?"

"No, but maybe that is for the best, Nathan," Madame Luiza sympathized.

"She's right. This way we can get past Amani's transition and Lillian will be better off meeting the Amani we all know and love, and not the one currently being manipulated by Khalida," Calla Lily added.

Nathan sighed, but agreed.

"Nathan, dear, would you mind running up to the inn and getting some firewood?" Madame Luiza asked. "You know where Mihail stacks it."

"Of course. I didn't realize we were running low," Nathan replied.

"I don't want the two of you to get a chill in the middle of the night," she added.

"I'll be back in a bit," Nathan said, heading for the door. "Do we need anything else?"

"I think that should do it for now."

Nathan nodded and closed the door behind him.

Calla Lily gave Madame Luiza a sideways glance. "It's not supposed to be too cold tonight."

"No, but I needed him to go so we could talk freely."

"About?"

"Do you hear anything unusual?'

Calla Lily furrowed her brows. "No. What should I be hearing?"

"There are three of us, and yet I hear four distinct heartbeats."

"What?" Calla Lily exclaimed as she tapped into her inner sight and used her Shuvani powers. "I thought I heard something earlier when I was near Amani, but I assumed it had something to do with Khalida influencing her."

"Do we dare ask?"

"I think after what we just found out from Thoth about the merging, we need to ask. I mean is it possible it's already begun? Maybe part of Khalida is already here with Amani."

"Well, there is only one way to find out," Madame Luiza said with a sigh.

The two of them walked in to where Amani was resting. The sound became clearer and more distinct. It was rapid and had a specific cadence.

"How are you feeling?" Calla Lily asked.

Amani gave a faint smile. "Better, but I'm still so sorry to have frightened everyone."

"I can't lie and say it wasn't unnerving. I thought if things continued, Mihail was going to have to build a whole new cottage," Calla Lily teased.

"Thankfully it didn't come to that," Amani said with a slight laugh that shifted into something more somber. "I would have wanted to die if I had hurt anyone here."

"We know, and it didn't come to that, so we're all free to move on," Calla Lily said, moving to sit on the edge of the bed next to Amani. "Can we ask you something now that it is just us?"

Amani nodded. "Absolutely. You can ask me anything."

Calla Lily looked at Madame Luiza and then back to Amani. "We can hear another heartbeat, and its rhythm is not your usual tempo. Madame Luiza and I wanted to ask if maybe some of Khalida transferred into you when you changed, and that is what we are hearing."

Amani's gaze dropped to her hands. "No, my sister—or whatever she is—has nothing to do with it." She met their curious stare. "I'm with child."

Madame Luiza and Calla Lily gasped and then burst into joyous praise.

"This is wonderful news," Calla Lily cooed.

"Yes, wonderful indeed. Have you told Nathan?"

Amani shook her head. "I just found out amidst all this chaos. Thoth told me. I guess I'm not doing a good job so far at being a mother, if you two were able to hear the heartbeat and I could not."

"Don't you dare say that. You've had quite a lot to contend with," Calla Lily insisted. "Would you mind if I read you? Madame Luiza can hear the little one much better than I, but I can sense it better through my sight."

"Thoth only said I was with child, nothing more. I hadn't had the chance to tell Nathan because, well, with everything—I don't know exactly how to tell him. What with Lillian here and all. What will she say at Nathan being a father before he is married? Isn't it the custom of humans to marry before they are in the family way?"

Madame Luiza scoffed. "Maybe, but you are not human, Amani. Nothing about you and Nathan will ever fall into the normal confines of the world."

Amani's face fell. "I want so much to fit in."

"Why, though, dear? You are unique, not only because of your djinn powers, but because you are a lovely, kind woman. You will be a wonderful mother. Motherhood is a blessing to be cherished," Madame Luiza lamented as she moved to sit on the other side of Amani.

Amani placed her hands on Madame Luiza's and Calla Lily's,

connecting the three of them. Together they went on a journey, watching as the energy from the baby drew their attention. The heart was fully formed and beating in a melodic rhythm, a radiating glow of pink and red, with casts of orange surrounding the little bundle. As they grew closer to the child through their mental connection, the baby turned to look at them. Peace and love radiated from her. Yes, she made herself known and smiled at them all. The moment slipped, and the three of them were suddenly back on the bed, staring at one another.

"Did you see that?" Amani beamed.

"It's a girl," Calla Lily cooed.

"I can't believe it. How wonderful was that? It's as if she knew we were there. Oh, I've never experienced anything like that," Madame Luiza raved.

"She's bigger than I assumed she would be. Doesn't it take longer for babies to grow in their mother's womb?" Amani asked.

"Well, that depends on when she was conceived," Calla Lily answered. "But, I think it's safe to say that your little girl is part djinn, and we may need to consult Thoth or Hathor about this. She's growing fast, which means you need to tell Nathan as soon as possible," Calla Lily said with a faint smile.

"I'm back," Nathan's voice boomed from the other room.

"Speak of the devil."

Amani's brows furrowed. "Oh no, Nathan is no devil. He's my angel."

Calla Lily and Madame Luiza chuckled.

"It's a saying, nothing more. People say it when they're talking about someone and then they show up," Madame Luiza explained.

"We should be going. We'll check in on you in the morning," Calla Lily said as she stood.

"You ladies okay?" Nathan asked as he popped his head into the bedroom. When Madame Luiza and Calla Lily moved to leave, Nathan frowned. "Don't leave on my account. I'm going to start a fire to warm the living room."

When they walked out of the room, a chill hit them, sending a shiver through them both. "Yes, it seems you do need to warm up this room."

"I don't get it. The temperature is at least ten degrees cooler in here than outside. I'll get it warmed up, though," Nathan said as he tossed a few logs into the stone fireplace.

"That is odd," Madame Luiza said, casting a curious glance at Calla Lily.

"Sleep well, Nathan," Calla Lily said as she and Madame Luiza made their way to the door.

"You as well. I will be up to the inn first thing to check on Lillian. She's an early riser, and I don't want you all to have to bother with her inquisition." He winked.

"She's no trouble, but I'm sure she'd rather see you than us at breakfast," Madame Luiza replied.

"I don't know. She seemed right at home with you ladies. It was like watching her with her knitting circle back home."

"Now, Nathan, we may seem like that, but you know we are so much more than *knitting circle* ladies," Madame Luiza said, something flashing over her grey-green eyes.

Nathan laughed out loud. "Please excuse my confusion. You are definitely not like her normal friends—I think you're more fun, though. Does that count?"

"For now," she teased, closing the door behind her.

As Calla Lily and Madame Luiza walked away from the cottage, the chill they felt in their bones eased with each step they took.

"What is that? Do you think Roman put a hex on the area?" Calla Lily asked, casting a glance back at the cottage. "I don't see anything, but there is definitely something lingering, and with Roman's remarks earlier about Amani, and then him seeing Thoth and me at the falls . . ." She trailed off.

"What comments, and why on earth would he hex the cottage? To what end?" Madame Luiza speculated.

"Why does Roman do anything?"

"I can have Mihail check with him. Or could it be Thoth's doing?" Madame Luiza asked.

Calla Lily shrugged. "At this point anything is possible."

"Do you want me to walk you home?" Madame Luiza offered.

"No, I'm fine. I'll stop by and see you tomorrow. Thank you for the offer, though."

Madame Luiza turned and headed toward the inn. "Until tomorrow then."

"Until tomorrow." Calla Lily waved before putting her hands in her pockets to warm them. Her fingers tingled when they made contact with her tarot cards. She pulled them out and there on top was the Empress card, face up, even though she remembered flipping it back over. "Everything is going to be just fine, Amani. You'll get your happily ever after in the end," she said under her breath, rounding the corner on her way home.

CHAPTER 12

*W*hen Khalida woke, Thoth was gone, but she could sense where he was—had felt it through Amani. Rage coursed through her veins at the thought of her sister.

"Why do I feel you now more than ever before?" she snarled. Amani did not respond, of course, but there was no doubt their connection had strengthened lately.

Ice crystals began to form on the hair of her arms almost in concert with the cold hatred she felt for Amani. Khalida watched as icicles continued to spread to every surface around her, wondering how it was possible and why she didn't feel the cold herself. When the process stopped, Khalida found her cage to be completely frozen. Khalida looked at the ice shards and smirked, thinking they could be useful in battle. The ice was different than her usual power. Typically, energy surged through her, until the intensity arced out of her and into whatever she chose as a target, but this—she twisted her hands and arms, admiring the icy crystals as they glistened—was intriguing. As she continued to admire the clear stalagmites, an odd sensation fluttered in Khalida's stomach, shifting her attention. She could feel movement and hear a faint thrumming rhythm. Shock resonated through her. It was a heartbeat. Amani was with child.

"NO!" Khalida screamed. "You do not get to have everything you want while I am here, trapped in Thoth's prison."

The rage and pain continued to surge. Amani had killed Khaldun and was now living her dream of being a wife and mother—it was all coming to fruition while Khalida's dreams were shattered as she awaited punishment. Waves of energy pulsed under Khalida's skin, building until the crystal shards covering her and the space around her exploded. The frozen cage was now filled with powdery bits, falling and floating from every direction while the walls remained intact. A fine snow blustered around her, hiding Khalida from view to anyone who would attempt to look in. It was the perfect camouflage as tears started to stream down her face.

"Tears?" Khalida cried out. "I refuse to feel your weakness, Amani. REFUSE!"

Ever since she was a young girl, she never understood why Amani would stop to help people who were suffering. Why she'd cry when they cried or laugh when they laughed. Khalida never felt any of those emotions. Even with Khaldun, it wasn't love she felt. Lust, passion, a shared desire to elicit pain in others—that was what drove them, bound them together. However, now she was feeling sentiment. Sorrow was now intermingled with joy, fear, and love for whatever was connected to the tiny movements within her. The sound of the heartbeat became a beacon for her to home in on. Then realization dawned and snapped her back to the truth of the situation. The child may not be hers, but with a *shift* or a *change*, it could be. She could be the one to emerge— no, she *would* be the one to emerge—as the dominant personality.

The air around Khalida warmed, clearing her vision and thawing everything around her. She wondered what other things she could *feel* or *manipulate* to her advantage. They were connected earlier, and that led to feeling more of Amani's emotions.

"Guess it's time to find out," she whispered, looking around to make sure there was no evidence of her glacial explosion. When she was certain there were no remnants to alert Thoth, she lay down in her bed and closed her eyes, dreaming of the life she'd take from Amani.

~

"HOW ARE YOU FEELING?" Nathan asked as he brought a cup of hot tea in to Amani.

"Much better. I just can't seem to shake this chill," she said, shivering.

"Here," he said, handing her the tea. "Let me get you an extra blanket."

Amani took a sip of the tea and moaned. "Oh, this so delicious. I can taste vanilla and the raspberries along with a tiny hint of mint."

"Well, that is rather specific. You can taste each one?" Nathan said as he brought the blanket over to Amani and covered her with it. "Why are your teeth chattering? Is the tea not warming you?"

"I can't shake the cold because it is not anything here in the cottage. It's Khalida's doing."

"How? What can we do to stop this?"

"There's nothing anyone can do until we merge. She's angry that I'm free and she is not," Amani said before she drank the last bit of tea. The cup was still warm, so she gripped it with both hands, hoping to steady the shaking. "The link between us is becoming more fluid."

"Can't you counteract her power by using your own?"

"I can, but I'm worried it may strengthen her, and I don't need her stronger. Besides, I don't want to anger the Court by using more of my magic."

Nathan shook his head. "No, we definitely don't need that," he said, sitting on the edge of the bed next to her and wrapping his hands around hers.

Amani gave him a somber smile. "I'm sorry I've become such a burden. I should've known better than to believe she'd allow me a moment of peace." Her eyes lowered to his hands on hers. "Especially after I killed Khaldun. I'm here with you, happy and moving on with life, and that is what she'll fight to destroy."

"You didn't have a choice. You did what you needed to do to save yourself and all of us."

"I know, but Khalida has never seen herself as others have. She's always believed that my goodness was my flaw . . . my weakness. She sees me as the one who needs to be removed, not her."

Nathan rubbed their hands together to create more warmth. "Well, that is not going to happen. I will not lose you now that I have finally found true happiness."

Amani's eyes lit up. "Nathan, I need to tell you something," she said softly. "I'm—"

Amani was unable to finish that sentence, however, because the mug she and Nathan were still gripping exploded. Shards went everywhere as the two of them were blown backwards by a massive blast. When Amani came to, she saw Nathan lying a distance away on the floor of the living room, motionless.

"Nathan," Amani screamed as she scrambled to him, lifting him into her arms. There was blood on his shirt, and he was unresponsive. "Please don't leave me. I love you and we're going to have a baby. Please, Nathan, please come back to me," she cried.

When Nathan remained silent, Amani's heart sank. She felt something wet on her fingers and lifted them up to see crimson coating her hand. Nathan was hurt worse than she knew. Amani cried out for Thoth, Hathor, Ma'at, and Calla Lily, anyone she could think of to help, but for the first time since this day started, they were alone. Amani closed her eyes and embraced her djinn. Using her power had brought the Court and others running every other time. She could only hope this would not be the exception. Amani's eyes were ablaze, but not the rest of her. She was managing to contain the surge, but knew Khalida would use this as a way to gain control. Maybe that was her plan all along. However, in this moment, nothing else mattered except saving Nathan.

Mihail, Irina, and Madame Luiza came through the cottage door in a blur and stopped the second they saw Nathan in Amani's arms.

"What happened?" Mihail asked, kneeling beside Amani.

"Khalida exploded the mug we were holding, and when I came to, he was like this," she said, showing him the blood on her hands.

Mihail inhaled deeply, pinpointing Nathan's head wound, then again moved in a blur. He'd grabbed a blade and drug it across his palm, quickly pouring his pooled blood down Nathan's throat. Silence filled the cottage as seconds turned to minutes, the others from the Court filtering in, until Nathan gasped and opened his eyes.

Nathan's eyes were wide and his skin pale. "Where's Amani? Is she okay?" Nathan croaked, his voice raspy and on edge.

Mihail, Irina, Madame Luiza, and Calla Lily were all speaking to him, telling him to lie still, that he'd need a minute and that he was okay, but Amani stood motionless, staring at him. Nathan propped himself up on his elbow and peered at her.

"What's wrong with her?" Nathan asked.

They all turned to look at Amani, Mihail moving to instantly shield Nathan. They stared as her hair turned black, with long white strands flowing down past her arms. Her skin was pale, almost blue, and her now opaque eyes were staring blankly at Nathan.

"You were supposed to have died. Too bad. I'll get you eventually." Her voice was harsh and not her own.

"That's not Amani," Saundra offered before tossing a spell bottle at Amani's feet.

Amani's head twisted toward Saundra. "You have no power or dominion over me, witch."

"No, but I do," a baritone voice said from the bedroom doorway.

Everyone turned their attention to Thoth. With a snap of his fingers, Amani fell to the floor, and Calla Lily rushed to her side. As she held Amani in her arms, she changed back to the woman they knew, but she didn't wake. Calla Lily fixed her gaze on the God of Wisdom. "Care to explain what the hell that was and why Nathan almost died tonight?"

"The simple answer is, we are not going to be able to wait until the new moon to merge Amani and Khalida." He turned to Nathan. "What happened in there tonight?" he asked, pointing to the bedroom.

Nathan quickly recounted everything up to the mug exploding. "I don't remember anything else after that."

"Amani opened herself up to embrace her djinn to try to save Nathan," Mihail interjected. "After feeling her magic, we all arrived, and I used my blood to save Nathan, but have no idea how much time passed before Khalida took over Amani's body."

"Their connection has become stronger lately, and they're feeding off of one another," Thoth replied.

"Amani said she wouldn't use her djinn power to fight Khalida's link because she thought it may strengthen her," Nathan said, sitting up with Mihail's help.

"Nathan, was anything happening to Amani before all this transpired?" Thoth asked.

"She was freezing. I just thought she was cold until she said it was Khalida's doing."

"It's been cold here in the house, too," Madame Luiza said. "Calla Lily and I noticed it before we left earlier."

"I can feel a presence too," Saundra offered. "It's gone now, though." She turned to Roman. "Are you getting anything?"

"No, but there's no denying the power behind what we just saw," Roman answered with narrowed eyes and a flexing jaw.

Thoth nodded. "She plans to divide you all and make you hurt one another. She's using Amani to achieve her goals."

"And why should we believe that Amani is not a part of it?" Roman snapped.

Thoth turned to face him. "Your need to make Amani the villain is acknowledged, but not verified. I've explained that they are not twins but two halves of a whole. Once the two parts are reunited, you will see the truth."

"And if you're wrong?"

"I'm never wrong."

Calla Lily bit back a grin but focused on Amani. "What can we do for Amani in the meantime?"

"The best choice is for her to return with me, but I know that won't be acceptable to you. I'll return tomorrow," Thoth replied, then flicked his wrist, causing Amani to float up and out of Calla Lily's arms, hovering midair. "She'll need to rest and not be agitated in any way. That's what gives Khalida the opening she needs to take over. Don't give it to her." Thoth cast a quick glance at Roman. With another flick of his wrist, Thoth led a still hovering, still unconscious, Amani to the bedroom and laid her down gently before returning to the kitchen where everyone was still standing.

"I've never seen anything like that," Nathan said with a quick shake of his head. "I know Roman has reservations about Amani being here, Thoth, but I'm telling you, she has no ill intentions toward anyone. Just tell us what is needed to get her back to herself, and we will make it happen . . . all of us," he said confidently, looking to the others.

Roman sneered while the rest nodded in agreement.

"The task will be more difficult now, but we can manage it. I've informed Hathor and Ma'at of the situation, and they are already preparing what Amani will need," Thoth said, looking at Calla Lily.

"What are you two not telling us?" Roman questioned. "You both were at the falls having a private discussion, and now there is something unspoken in your exchange. If you expect my cooperation, you'll divulge your plan—now."

"I don't expect your cooperation. I expect your compliance." Thoth glared at Roman. "I will not answer for anything. You will help to save yourself. And you'll help to save Havenwood Falls. Otherwise Khalida will take over a weakened Amani, and she'll kill you all." Thoth turned his attention back to the rest of the group. "I'm not asking for your help. I'm demanding it for the sake of us all. We can stop a tragedy by joining together and working as one. Are the rest of you willing?"

Nods and collective yeses followed, and Roman reluctantly included his agreement with a huff.

"When the sun begins to set, the goddesses and I will be by the water's edge near the falls. Bring what is needed, and we will finally be rid of this once and for all." Thoth nodded at Calla Lily, another unspoken conversation between the two of them, but one Calla Lily acknowledged with a nod of her own.

"We will be ready," she said, just before Thoth vanished in a wisp of sand.

"You never cease to amaze me with your ability to anger people, Roman. You decide to go toe to toe with a god?" Calla Lily said, shaking her head. "Saundra, should you go talk to the rest of the Court?"

"It's the middle of the night."

"I know, but it seems we have a clock ticking and much to be done." Irina grabbed a piece of paper and fountain pen out of the drawer and handed it to Calla Lily. "Make us a list of what we need."

Calla Lily scribbled on the page. "Madame Luiza and I will take care of Amani. Irina and Mihail can keep an eye on Nathan, and soon this will all be over and we can get back to our normal, boring everyday lives."

"What about Lillian?" Nathan interjected.

Calla Lily blew out an exhausted breath. "In all this chaos, I completely forgot she was here."

"The wards will keep the magic from her, but the Luna Coven will make certain she stays safe but unaware," Saundra offered.

"Thank you, Saundra."

"So, we have a plan?" Mihail asked, looking at the group.

"So it seems," Roman quipped.

"We'll meet tomorrow morning at nine at the inn to make sure we are all ready," Mihail said, taking Irina's hand in his. "Nathan, take it easy tonight. My blood healed you, but you almost died, and we're going to have a lot to do tomorrow to prepare."

"Yes, sir," Nathan replied. "And thank you. Thank you for saving me and for allowing Amani and me to stay here. We never meant to cause any harm."

"We know, Nathan. We're fond of you both, and like Calla Lily said, this will be over soon." Mihail extended his hand to Nathan.

Nathan shook his hand, then watched as everyone but Calla Lily and Madame Luiza left.

Calla Lily turned to Nathan. "Go be with her. I'm going to sleep at the inn tonight just in case anything else should happen. That way we're all close. We don't know what tomorrow night will bring, so talk to her and then get some sleep."

Nathan complied, leaving Madame Luiza and Calla Lily alone in the kitchen.

"Amani didn't get the chance to tell him about the baby, that's what was unspoken between you and Thoth, wasn't it?" Madame Luiza asked as she picked up the list and started to move toward the door.

"Yes, the baby adds a wrinkle, but with a binding, we can save them both. I'd like for Amani to be the one to tell him and not have him find out he's going to be a father while everything is happening."

"Oh, dear. This is an impossible situation, it seems. I adore them, but life has been a little too exciting for my taste since they arrived," Madame Luiza said as she and Calla Lily walked out of the cottage.

"We'll be begging for some excitement after they're gone, I'm sure," Calla Lily joked.

CHAPTER 13

$\mathscr{A}$mani sat up and stared down at her tattered and torn dress. Tears welled in her eyes as she looked at the blood—Nathan's blood. She almost lost him tonight and knew Khalida would stop at nothing to make her as miserable as she was. Amani remembered the threat she'd made over the centuries, that she'd kill them both to save the ones she loved. However, now it was Khalida making the threats and turning them into actions. The problem Amani faced, though, was that she couldn't follow through with her threat, because it would kill her child, and that was something she would never do.

"How am I going to fix this?" Amani said under her breath as she undressed.

As she stood in her slip, she ran her hands over her belly and promised to keep her baby safe at all cost. Amani bent down and picked up the clothes and folded them neatly. She pulled the comb out of her hair and let her blond curls spill over her shoulders.

"If you'd only stayed locked away, then none of this would've happened," Amani said aloud.

Just then, Nathan walked into the bedroom. "If you'd only stayed locked away, then I would never know what love felt like," he answered as the door clicked closed.

"Oh, you startled me."

Nathan walked over to her, but stopped short. "You are so beautiful," he said, stepping closer and taking her hand in his, "even with soot on your cheeks."

Amani shook her head. "I'd assume beautiful would be the last word to describe me tonight."

"What's wrong?" he said, pulling a handkerchief out of his pocket and using it to wipe her face. "I know Khalida is causing you trouble, but I feel like there is something else bothering you."

Her eyes flashed to his. "There is something I've been wanting to tell you, but all these things keep happening and . . ."

He kissed her forehead gently and then her lips. "Want to tell me now? It's just us."

Amani rose up on the balls of her feet, her hands on his cheeks, and captured his lips. The kiss spoke a thousand words, but not the ones she most needed to say. When she broke their kiss, Nathan was dazed as he stared at her.

"I cannot believe I almost lost you," she whispered.

"But you didn't. I'm right here."

Amani met his eyes. "I love you, Nathan."

He smiled down at her. "I love you, too."

Amani glanced down, but then finally blurted, "I was going to tell you earlier . . . before the . . . but then everything—"

"What is it?" Nathan said softly, sensing her nervousness.

"I think I'd rather show you."

"Okay." A grin played at his lips as he looked down at the nude silk slip she was wearing.

Amani reached for his hand. "Do you remember when we first connected?" Nathan nodded, and she continued, "It's been unintentional, but I've been blocking our link. I've had to disconnect myself so Khalida couldn't get to you, but what I need you to know is too important."

"I thought something felt off with us, but assumed it was because of all you were having to deal with. I can still feel our connection, though. It's just faint."

"From now on it will only become stronger."

He cocked his head and reached for a lock of her hair. "Okay."

Amani linked their fingers and let all she needed, no, *wanted* him to know flow from her to him with ease. Gold tendrils wound down her hands and made their way into his. They coiled and snaked up his arms and headed straight for his heart.

Nathan sucked in a harsh breath at the sensation.

"It's okay, just breathe. I'm here."

The tendrils changed and formed into hieroglyphs, then returned to lines flowing through his veins. Amani was sending him her every thought, every joy, every passion, and every pain she'd ever endured. Nathan stared down at her, feeling every emotion, every bit of her essence until they came to a single moment—the first time they made love. He pulled her closer as they watched themselves intertwined and full of passion.

Nathan lifted Amani and carried her over to the bed, their fingers still linked, their bond surging. He laid her down gently, hovering above her as the images of them making love continued to replay. The way he let his fingers roam over the soft contours of her skin. The way she arched her back when he felt her warmth on his fingers for the first time. Every second was tingling on his skin until it felt as if they were actually doing it right then.

Amani moaned, and Nathan pressed his lips to hers, pausing only a moment to whisper, "I loved our first time together, but we don't have to relive it in a dream. I'd be happy to show you just how much I love you right now if you want."

"But you needed to see this first time to know what I needed to show you," she replied between his kisses.

Nathan stopped when something ignited between them. Gold and crimson merging in a tornadic swirl, changing and shifting—exploding, until the soft sound of a heartbeat clicked. Nathan watched as a glow he'd not seen until now radiated from her. Nathan continued to watch the spark turn into a bundle and then move to face them, her soft features coming into focus.

"A baby? Ours?" Nathan stammered.

Amani nodded, and Nathan kissed her again.

"Is she a djinn like you?"

"She's a bit of both of us, and I honestly don't know what she will be."

"Well, just like with you, I will take her as she is and be grateful for the gift. Oh Amani, I'm so happy."

"I wanted you to see how we created life. How the love we share made something special and unique."

"Well, you did more than that," he teased, "but I don't know what to say other than I love you."

"I didn't know if you'd be upset. We're not married, and I know how much it means for human couples to be bound in such a way."

"Amani, all I care about is that you love me and you're mine. The rest, we can figure out later. Your life, your health—" he slid his hand over her belly—"and this baby are all that matter to me. We'll have plenty of time later to figure out titles and social mores."

Amani ran her hand up Nathan's chest and caressed his cheek. "Make love to me," she breathed. "I don't know what tomorrow will bring, but I refuse to lose any more time with you, Nathan."

Nathan didn't think about a response; instead, he acted. Neither of them needed to think about tomorrow in this moment. All they needed was to embrace their desire for one another, making love until they were both spent.

THE FIRE WAS NOW a slow crackle in the room, the amber glow flickering on the ceiling as Amani lay draped over Nathan's chest. She ran her fingers over his heart, her thoughts a steady flow from her to him.

"I know you're nervous about tomorrow, but I will not let anything happen to you—you or the baby," Nathan reassured.

"I know, but Khalida knows about her too now, and she wants to be the one to surface and raise our child." Amani sighed.

"And from all I gathered from the group and Thoth, all

contingencies have been accounted for. You're going to be fine—we all are."

Amani sat up, wrapping the sheet around her chest.

"Are you getting cold? I can add more wood to the fire."

"Would you mind?"

"Not at all," Nathan said, slipping into his trousers before he headed into the main room.

When he returned, he tossed two logs into the hearth, then used the iron poker to stoke the fire. When the new logs began to burn, he walked back over to their bed and sat on the edge next to Amani.

"Can I get you anything? Water? Something to eat?"

She shook her head and blurted, "Can I ask you something?"

"Of course."

"I know that no matter what, I will always be yours. I want to bind us with more than just our thoughts. I want to make certain that Khalida cannot corrupt our love. Will you help me ask Hathor for her blessing to bind our union?"

"Yes." Nathan reached for her hand. "How do we ask her?"

Amani took Nathan's other hand in hers and turned them both until they were palms up. "In a reverent prayer," she answered, adding her hands to the top of his. "Goddess, I know I've asked for so much, and now I am asking again. You've blessed Nathan and me with a gift of the highest honor, and we humbly ask for one more wish to be granted. Release me from this curse and show Nathan and me how to bond together to defeat Khalida, so we can raise our daughter in peace."

They sat in silence, waiting, until a white feather appeared above their heads, then floated down to land softly in their outstretched hands. The feather burst into flames but was still cool against their palms. What remained was a golden feather on a matching chain.

"Isn't that your mother's necklace, the one you used to summon Hathor in the town square?"

"It is," she said, trying to choke back her emotions.

A voice, soft and gentle, spoke as if it were part of the air around them. "You have my blessing. You will need the union to ground yourselves tomorrow. I am pleased. You two are well suited."

Amani stared at Nathan as she offered her gratitude for this blessing. "Thank you, Goddess."

Nathan stammered, unsure of what to say or do, but he followed suit by thanking Hathor as well. "I promise to love her until the day we can both walk the duat together," he said out loud, his eyes never leaving Amani's.

"Very well."

The gold necklace twisted and coiled like Amani's blood until it knotted itself around both of their wrists. A searing pain burned where the golden cord was bound. "Forever until the end, you two shall be one."

The two of them watched as the necklace melded into their skin. The only visible evidence that it even existed was the faint markings on them both. Moments passed and the two just sat there, transfixed. Their thoughts had become one—they were in perfect harmony. Amani and Nathan went to release their hands but stopped when they felt something underneath their forearms. They watched as hieroglyphs appeared in a single row. It began at their wrists and moved toward their elbows—an ankh, the Eye of Horus, an image of Ma'at with her wings colorful and outstretched, followed by Hathor and Thoth's hieroglyphs. The final image to appear was a blue water lily. Nathan had seen these many times and nodded appreciatively. It was an important symbol in ancient Egypt, representing creation and rebirth —an homage to their child and Amani's merging. They had Hathor's blessing, and were now forever marked for all who dared to question the union between them.

"Thank you," Nathan said appreciatively. "I will not disappoint you. I will care for them both. Always."

Amani leaned forward and kissed Nathan. "Thank you for choosing me. I am the one who is honored."

The baby moved, and Nathan and Amani both laughed. They now felt everything together and would forever feel each other's thoughts and emotions, pain and joy.

"I think she wants to be included," Nathan chuckled. "Not even here and already demanding to be heard."

Nathan lay down, and Amani curled into him, laying her head on his chest. Her eyes grew heavy, and she once again thanked the goddesses and Thoth for their blessings before falling asleep. Nathan closed his eyes and listened to the sound of his daughter's and Amani's heartbeats until he too fell asleep. The three of them would be a family forever, bound through love.

CHAPTER 14

*N*athan was up early and got ready before Amani woke. He leaned down and kissed her forehead before he left to go meet with Calla Lily, Mihail, Irina, and Madame Luiza at the inn. With everything that happened last night, Nathan knew he didn't need to leave her a note, because she'd already know where he was when she thought of him. He left the cottage quietly and made his way to the inn's backdoor. He grabbed a handful of the firewood he chopped a few days ago and was headed for the parlor, but ran into Madame Luiza in the kitchen.

"You're up early," Madame Luiza said when she saw Nathan. "Are you hungry, dear?"

"Starving."

"Almost dying can do that to you," she teased. "How's Amani?"

"Still sleeping," he said as he lifted the wood in his arms. "I thought I'd bring in some wood for the hearth and meet with you all before bothering her. She's exhausted."

Madame Luiza focused on the eggs she was cracking. "When we're finished here this morning, I will send you home with a plate for her. Calla Lily said she'd be downstairs by eight."

"Did someone say my name?"

Madame Luiza laughed. "Good morning. Did you sleep well?"

"As best as I could," Calla Lily said, moving toward the tea kettle. "Do you mind?"

"Not at all. Help yourself," Madame Luiza responded. "Saundra and the rest of the Court aren't due here for another hour or so. That should be enough time to feed the guests, clean up, and gather the items we need."

"I'm happy to help with anything. Amani too, once she wakes," Nathan offered as he added the wood to the pile next to the stove. "What can I do in the meantime?"

When Nathan moved to shift the wood on the rack, his new hieroglyphs peeked out from under his sleeve, catching Calla Lily's eye.

"Did you and Amani have a chance to speak last night?" she said, gesturing to Madame Luiza to look at Nathan's arm as he rearranged the wood so it wouldn't fall.

"Yes, we spoke," Nathan said nonchalantly as he continued to stack. "And yes, I know you both know."

A grin tipped Madame Luiza's lips as she whisked the eggs. "Then it's safe to offer our congratulations."

The tea kettle whistled, and Calla Lily pulled it off of the fire to let it cool while she put two pinches of fresh lavender over the top of some green tea leaves. She grabbed an orange from the basket on the butcher block and begun to peel it as Nathan rolled up his sleeves and showed her and Madame Luiza the markings.

"Amani and I have the same hieroglyphs. We connected our lifelines to one another with Hathor's blessing. We are one."

"We're happy for you both," Calla Lily said as she looked over at Madame Luiza.

"I don't know what those mean, Nathan, but a blessing from Egyptian gods is a wonder in and of itself," Madame Luiza stated.

"It will serve us all tonight that you are linked to her," Calla Lily said, placing the peel in the bottom of her cup before reaching for the kettle. The scent of orange and lavender filled the kitchen as the hot water hit the ingredients, overriding the smell of the biscuits cooking in the oven. "Anyone else want a cup?"

Madame Luiza went to answer, but the bell chimed, and she turned toward the sound. "Duty calls. I will have to get one later."

"I can check on that, Madame Luiza, and you can finish the eggs and enjoy a cup of tea," Nathan offered.

"That would be great. Can you check with Irina, too, and see how many guests we'll be having down for breakfast?"

"Sure thing," Nathan said, grabbing the notepad Madame Luiza used to write down the food orders. "Amani is awake, by the way, if you needed to speak with her."

"How do you . . ." Calla Lily asked.

"She just said good morning, and that she'll be over to help us soon." Nathan winked.

Madame Luiza stirred the eggs on the stove and shrugged. "Seems you have some supernatural abilities of your own now, Nathan. Now go and get those orders for me. These eggs will be finished in a minute, and so will the biscuits."

Nathan gave her a quick nod and headed out of the kitchen. When he rounded the corner, he stopped short.

"Nathan, where have you been? I thought I was having breakfast with you and Amani this morning," Lillian said, moving to hug him. "You're not dressed for a meal."

"I'm sorry, Lillian," he replied as he embraced her. "I completely forgot, and Amani is still resting. How about just the two of us?" he offered, leading her into the dining room. "I am helping Madame Luiza with the breakfast, but as soon as I'm finished, I'll be all yours."

"You've always been a helper. I'll be here." She lifted her book. "I have a few more pages, and I'll be finished."

Nathan pulled the chair out for her. "Would you like coffee or tea this morning?"

"Coffee would be wonderful."

"Breakfast will be ready in a bit."

An older couple and their daughter walked into the dining room, and Nathan made sure to mark down what they'd like to drink before heading to the lobby to check in with Irina. "Good morning."

"Good morning to you. You look well rested. How is Amani?"

"Amani and I slept well, thank you."

"Is she feeling better? Mihail and I have been worried about you both."

"She's feeling much better and is looking forward to getting tonight over with so we can move on with our lives."

"And the baby?" Irina beamed.

"You knew?"

"Mihail and I heard the heartbeat, and then Madame Luiza and Calla Lily confirmed it. We're happy for you both."

Nathan nodded. "Thank you. I'm a blessed man to have them both."

Irina gestured toward Lillian. "And don't worry. We'll keep the secret. No one else need know until you and Amani are ready to tell it."

"Good morning, Nathan. It is nice to see you up and around. Can you tell Madame Luiza we'll be having six guests for breakfast?" Mihail called out, putting him back on task.

"I can do that," Nathan said before he turned to leave. He stopped short, though, and turned back to face Mihail and Irina. "I don't know how I will ever be able to thank you for saving my life last night. I'll forever be indebted to you." He ducked his head. "All of you."

"No need to thank me. I've grown to like you, Nathan." Mihail smiled. "Can't imagine the world without you a part of it."

Words caught in Nathan's throat, and he gave Mihail and Irina a quick nod before heading back into the kitchen.

The next hour flew by, and all the guests were taken care of and had moved on with their day. All except Lillian. Nathan had stopped by her table several times to offer apologies and more coffee, but he could tell she was growing tired of him coming and going. Amani had sensed his agitation and came to help in the kitchen so he could finally entertain Lillian, though it quickly became obvious he was failing in his duty.

"Nathan, did you even hear a word I said?"

"What?" he stammered. "I'm sorry, Lillian. I was distracted."

"By what?" she said, before following his sightline and realizing why in an instant.

There in the doorway was Amani. Her blond hair fell over her shoulders in soft curls, and the pale gray dress she was wearing made her look ethereal. Lillian watched as Amani and Nathan stared at one another as if they'd known each other for a lifetime. Love and peace radiated from them both, and Lillian's heart swelled. The boy she'd taken care of for so long, the young man who'd endured years of suffering, had finally found joy. Nathan stood and walked over to Amani.

He intertwined their fingers and tucked her arm under his. "You look beautiful."

Amani blushed and leaned in closer to Nathan. "You say that all the time. Soon I will start to believe it."

Nathan kissed her cheek and led her over to the couch where Lillian was now sitting.

"I'd like to apologize for last night. I wasn't feeling well and needed to go rest. I hope you enjoyed your evening, Lillian."

"Nothing to worry about, dear. I know how to amuse myself when company is absent," she insisted. "It gave me a chance to read my book, and for that, I am grateful."

"Did you enjoy it?" Amani asked.

"Very much. Would you care to read it? I can give it to you, and you can read it at your leisure," Lillian offered.

Amani glanced at Nathan before she smiled at Lillian. "That would be lovely. Thank you."

Calla Lily came into the parlor with a tray in her hand. It had a floral teapot, several matching cups, and a pile of cookies on a plate.

"Anyone for tea?" she asked. "Madame Luiza sent out some homemade oatmeal cookies, too."

"I love oatmeal cookies," Lillian responded.

"Lillian, I'd like you to meet Saundra Beaumont. She lives here in Havenwood Falls," Nathan said, standing when Saundra walked in a few steps behind Calla Lily.

Saundra regarded Nathan and Amani as she moved to sit next to

Lillian. "Calla Lily was asking for the two of you to assist with some tasks in the kitchen. I'll be more than happy to entertain Lillian for a few minutes."

"Very well," Nathan said, leaning over to kiss Lillian on the cheek. "I'll find you when we're done."

"No rush," she answered. "I can't wait to pick Miss Beaumont's brain about this wonderful town. I overheard some of the other guests talking about the Great Falls and how majestic they were. It sounded wonderful."

"They are. We'll see you soon, then," Amani added before she and Nathan walked out of the room.

Gathered in the dining room were Mihail, Irina, Madame Luiza, Ric, and the remaining members of the Court. Calla Lily walked in a second later, followed by the pixies of the Spring Fae Court: Aeiri, Ushka, Tierri, and Enya. Amani squeezed Nathan's hand.

"It's all going to be all right," he said into her mind.

Ric turned to Calla Lily. "Where do we start? Gaby and Conall are awaiting word, and everyone in support of Nathan and Amani is ready to help with what we need to gather."

Calla Lily fiddled with the bracelets at her wrist. "Saundra has reinforced the wards and is taking care of watching Lillian and the other guests to keep everyone safe, so I think we're ready to get started."

Amani stepped away from Nathan and moved closer to the group. "I'd like to say something first." Everyone turned to look at her. "When I addressed you all last time, I said I would honor you and that I was at your service. Since then, I've done everything in my power to keep my word. I never meant to bring any harm to Havenwood Falls, but I'm once again needing your help." She bent her head and sighed. "As it was before, I will not let Khalida hurt anyone and will sacrifice myself if it comes to that. All I ask is that you take care of Nathan, if the need arises."

Mihail spoke first. "We will not be losing any of you."

"No, not one," Irina added.

Amani turned to face Roman. "I know we have conflict, but I need not be your enemy," she stated.

"I wouldn't consider you one if you didn't feel the need to keep secrets."

"Even you have your secrets, Roman. I am no different. However, the question you are dying to know the answer to is small in comparison to what we are about to face. I promise you that I am not a concern, but if you don't look at the bigger picture, Khalida most certainly will be." She extended her hand to him. "Peace for now?"

Roman narrowed his eyes and reluctantly extended his hand to meet hers. "For now."

With the pleasantries out of the way, the group went about making a plan. Each person had a task, and with the hours dwindling until sunset, there was no time to waste.

"Gather everything and meet at the water's edge at seven thirty," Calla Lily finished. "Be well until then."

CHAPTER 15

*A*t times the day seemed to drag on, while other times it seemed to speed up. Either way, everyone had been working diligently to gather all that was needed. As the sun began to dip in the sky, Amani changed into the dress she wore when she first arrived in Havenwood Falls. Thoth had requested that everyone be dressed in white to perform the merging because it symbolized power, purity, and simplicity—all traits important to their success.

The sky was changing from azure blue to varying shades of coral and magenta. The sun was setting, and the time was drawing near. Amani walked out into the garden and ran her hands delicately over the heather, watching as the season's last white and purple blooms swayed in the breeze.

"You should pick some and put it in your pocket," Calla Lily said softly.

Amani turned and gave her a half smile. "I hate picking them. I can feel their sadness at the loss of not being connected to the earth."

"I understand, but I think under the circumstances, they'd want to be with you."

"Why is that?"

"Heather is used to cleanse and protect. It also is used for good luck," Calla Lily said as she knelt beside the plant. "Will you offer your gifts to us this day?" The shrub bent forward, as if it were acknowledging Calla Lily's request. "Thank you," she answered as she snipped just what she would need for Amani.

She wrapped it with a piece of white muslin and handed it to Amani.

"I'm scared," Amani admitted as she took the floral bundle. "I can feel something stirring, and it reeks of ambiguity."

"Everything is going to be fine."

Amani took Calla Lily's hand. "I need you to promise me something."

"Of course. Anything."

"Protect Nathan and the baby no matter what happens," Amani pleaded.

Calla Lily's features hardened, and her eyes started to well with emotion. "I promise."

"I'm connected to Nathan. He knows and feels all that I do now that our lifelines are linked, but the baby is still too small and too vulnerable. Khalida will try to use her to break me."

"We won't let her," Calla Lily insisted.

"I've asked too much of you already, but there is no one other than Nathan that I trust more, and since he is human and you are Shuvani, I must ask one more thing," Amani said, her voice unwavering. "Will you link your bloodline to hers, so in the event something happens to me, she will have a tether to this world?"

"Oh, Amani. Have you talked to Nathan about this?"

"He knows it now that I've said it to you, and while he refuses to accept any outcome other than all of us together, he also understands he'd be powerless against Khalida. You and Thoth could save her."

Calla Lily lifted her chin and steadied her resolve as she took Amani's hands in hers. "I will do whatever you ask. I know we've only known one another a short time, but you are like a sister to me, and I will protect you and your daughter with all the power in my bloodline."

The two women embraced one another and sobbed, a golden white light surrounding them until they were of one mind. Like

Nathan and Amani, Calla Lily and Amani were linked through a magical bond—part djinn, part Shuvani.

"That little girl has one strong heartbeat, and if she is anything like her parents, she will be a force to be reckoned with," Calla Lily whispered.

"I agree," Nathan said from behind them.

Amani and Calla Lily broke their hug, and the three of them linked hands.

"Love and truth will rise above the darkness threatening to consume us," Amani avowed.

"Love and truth will rise," Nathan and Calla Lily repeated.

"Are you two ready to go?" Nathan asked. "It's time for us to head over."

The three of them made their way down the long path and onto the lane toward the Great Falls. When they arrived, Roman, Ric, Gaby, Conall, Mihail, Irina, Madame Luiza, and Saundra all stood in a pure white circle of light.

"We're waiting for Elsmed and the rest of the Court to join us. Then we will be ready," Saundra stated.

Tierri and Ushka skittered near Amani and moved to hug her before rushing away when the others suddenly appeared. Everyone was here. It was time.

Thunder cracked, and lightning burst open the sky as the distinctive aroma of frankincense filled the air. Another flash went from sky to ground, and Thoth appeared where the bolt was struck. Next to him were two rectangular stone sarcophagi, ruddy in color and etched in hieroglyphs. Thoth looked in the direction of the group and tilted his head in acknowledgement.

"You all look well this night," he announced.

The group offered welcoming greetings of their own as they stepped closer.

"What are these for?" Roman asked.

"These are for Amani and Khalida. Identical in every way except for the symbols etched into the surfaces."

"Why the difference?" Ric asked.

"Each is represented by their traits, and yet Amani's is unique because hers features Havenwood Falls and a symbol for each of you here to support her," Thoth said as he walked to the water's edge. "May I?"

Elsmed nodded. "Of course."

Thoth scooped up a handful of water and walked it over to Amani's sarcophagus. He let the aether-filled water spill onto the surface, and everyone watched as it lit up in vibrant colors. The sides and the top were covered in symbols and markings, each telling a story.

Nathan knelt down and studied the writing. "This is unbelievable. It's coming to life as the water reaches the symbols."

"And it will continue to change and evolve as Amani changes and evolves into the true nature of who she was meant to be."

Amani bowed her head to Thoth. "What do I need to do?"

"I will need you to lie here," he pointed. "Nathan, you will be by her feet to ground her, and Calla Lily, I will need you to stand by her head, to *guide* her."

"And the rest of us?" Mihail asked.

"The wolves would be best suited on the outer perimeter," Thoth suggested. "And the pixies will be helpful here by the water's edge, in case we need anything."

Ric, Gaby, and Conall wished everyone well and took off toward the forest, while the pixie sisters found a spot away from the stone monuments but close enough to be of service.

"And us?" Roman asked.

Thoth moved his hands in the air, and an ankh emblazoned itself in the sky above them. "A barrier that includes this would be most useful."

Saundra, Roman, and the rest of the Court made their way into their positions, the witches drawing on the others' magical energies to enchant the area surrounding the water. Another thunderous clap and a forked bolt of lightning struck near the water's edge. Hathor and Ma'at towered over everyone, until they noticed Thoth and transformed into a human stature that was much less intimidating.

The jackal guards who'd arrived just after the goddesses maintained their towering height.

"Goddesses," Amani said, bowing in reverence as they made their way over to where the sarcophagi were positioned.

"Amani." Hathor smiled. "You and Nathan look well."

"Thank you again. Your blessing was more than either of us could ever have asked for," she replied.

Ma'at looked at them both curiously, but when she saw the markings on Nathan and Amani's arms, she plucked a single blue feather from her ceremonial cloak and motioned for the two of them to come closer.

"When the day comes and we meet again in the Hall of Two Truths, remind me of this moment by returning this to me," Ma'at declared. "You have my blessing in this union."

The blue feather flew into the air and transformed into a million sparkling lights that shimmered like magical birds before landing softly on Nathan and Amani's forearms, joining their other markings. Nathan took Amani's hand, and they both knelt before the three gods.

Nathan pulled his father's pocket watch out, the chain jingling as he held it out for Thoth. "I know it is customary to offer a gift, and I am woefully unprepared, but this is my most treasured possession. I give it to you freely in gratitude for giving me something far more precious."

Thoth took the watch from Nathan. "Exquisite piece," he said, looking at it more closely. "A pillar verge fuse, and in perfect working condition, I might add." He looked back to Nathan. "Why is this your most treasured possession?"

"It was my father's."

"I see. The same father who made meeting Amani possible, yes?"

"Yes."

"Samuel honored my forty-two laws, and when his time came to be judged, his heart was lighter than a feather. He walks in peace. I thought you should know," Ma'at interjected.

A small gasp came from Nathan before he closed his eyes, struggling to compose himself. Thoth shook the watch to regain his attention. "You know, if you listen closely, this sounds exactly like the rhythm of your daughter's heartbeat," Thoth suggested.

Nathan nodded. "I know. It's almost as if one is connected to the other," he replied.

"Maybe they are," Thoth insinuated, "but for now, you keep this and let's get on with what we came here to do. Khalida is growing restless now that she is so close to Amani." Thoth handed the watch back to Nathan.

"Where is she?" Amani asked.

Thoth swirled his hands in the air and materialized a glass bottle with a brass neck, spout, and base. They all stared as the bottle seemed to pulse and shimmer with a pale blue light, as if an enchanted liquid were churning within.

"She's here," he said as he held the decanter in his hand.

"In the Prison of Asria?" Amani asked in a whisper. "But . . ."

Thoth gestured for Amani to lie down. "Is everyone ready?" Resounding yeses came from various parts of the space they were all occupying. "Then let's begin."

Amani lay down with her head closest to Calla Lily, while Nathan stood by her feet. Thoth stood next to her, between the two sarcophagi, and the goddesses stood at either end of the place where Khalida was to be laid out. Amani cast a glance at the stone slab next to her and wondered why Thoth had not used the water to activate the hieroglyphs on it. Was hers supposed to be dark and etched in black?

As if he reading her thoughts, he leaned down and whispered, "Light and dark, remember? You are the one we want to come forth, while she is to merge into the shadows." Amani nodded. "Now close your eyes and let me free you both."

Amani did as she was asked, but sent loving messages to both Nathan and Calla Lily before she closed her eyes.

"Out of the darkness there will be light," Thoth began.

"Be true of heart and weigh the cost of your actions against your love and truth," Ma'at added.

"This night, we right a wrong and bring peace to a lost soul," Hathor finished.

Amani could hear chanting and then the sound of something wet spilling onto rock. She didn't open her eyes for fear she'd disrupt the process, but the sound of thunder booming overhead startled her. Nathan sent images into her mind to help soothe her agitation. Khalida was now lying motionless next to her. Thoth was doing something Nathan didn't understand but assumed was part of the progression needed to perform the merging.

"Amani, it is time to embrace your djinn," Thoth commanded. "Release who you are and allow all of you to be seen." Amani shivered at his words. "Don't worry. The fire that burns within you will not harm Calla Lily or Nathan. You must do this to allow the merge."

Amani did as instructed and embraced the side of her she had so desperately tried to keep hidden. Within a moment, her skin turned a dusky grey and her hair was ablaze. The sound that followed was gruesome. Khalida was awake, but bound and enraged. Amani could feel her trying to enter her thoughts, and when that didn't work, she tried other ways to take hold. First it was Amani's connection to Nathan, but Thoth had thwarted that. She then tried Calla Lily, but her Shuvani power sent Khalida searching for another link. She screamed again, a ghastly wail, but Amani held steady—that is, until Khalida went for the baby. Amani wrapped her arms around herself and curled into a ball. Thoth, Hathor, and Ma'at instantly reacted.

"Nathan," Thoth shouted, "your watch—give it to me."

Nathan fumbled in his pocket and handed it to Thoth. Nathan watched as the inner workings of the watch sprang to life in a far different way than he thought possible. First it stopped altogether, and he panicked, but then the watch whirred and clicked to life, beating faster than a hummingbird's wings.

Amani began to cry, and her body was turning cold. Her legs felt like ice, and Nathan held on for dear life as she continued to writhe in pain. Calla Lily's face turned pale, and he wondered why she was so shaken. Voices began to whisper and call to him. Nathan had been so focused on Amani's physical well-being that he stopped listening to her talk to him in his mind, but it seemed Calla Lily had heard every word.

"Calla Lily, please. I beg you. Help the baby. Khalida is taking her from me. I cannot bear to lose her. Please, please help my child."

Nathan stared at Calla Lily and then addressed Thoth. "Khalida is trying to kill the baby."

"No," Thoth snarled, moving back toward Khalida, but stopped when Calla Lily held her arms out wide. Tapping into the magic of her bloodline, and also that of the Court, power surged through her, and she used her thoughts to create her actions. The palm of her hand began to slice open, blood pooling where the cuts were visible. Calla Lily's hair blew wildly in the wind as she started to speak Romani. No one understood her except Nathan, thanks to their link with Amani, who heard her words clearly.

Blood to blood, bound to thee,
Guardian to child, accepted by three
Link us now, and forever remain
Protected by the Shuvani vein

When the last word was spoken, Calla Lily took her blood-soaked hands and laid them across Amani's womb. Amani gasped, and her body went slack.

"What's happened?" Thoth demanded.

Calla Lily's eyes opened in a rush. "I've protected the baby, but her heartbeat is dangerously weak. Khalida is now going for Amani. Save her!"

"No, save my baby," Amani pleaded, reaching for Thoth.

"I can only do one thing. I either save you, or I save the baby."

"The baby," Amani breathed. "I willingly give my life for hers. I will not let Khalida have her."

Thoth stood frozen for a moment, their lives in his hands. "Then again, perhaps there may be a way I can do both." His eyes snapped to Amani. "In order to succeed, I have to give the baby your power and you will end up human."

Tears spilled from Amani's eyes as she looked at Thoth and then Nathan, nodding as they silently made their decision. "The baby is our choice. Nathan and I will raise her until it is our time to answer to

Ma'at. Beyond that, Calla Lily and those in her line will guide our girl until we once again meet in the afterlife."

Calla Lily wiped Amani's forehead as beads of sweat pooled. "I promised you I would, and I will keep my promise."

Ma'at stepped over to Amani and touched her hand, reaching out for Nathan's as well. "It is my will that your lifelines will be bound. You are not only linked in life but so shall you be in death. Whomever dies first, the other will follow, so you may walk the duat side by side. This is my blessing to you both."

The air sizzled, and Thoth shot a look over at Khalida. Hathor and Ma'at could feel it too, and reached for Nathan while Thoth grabbed Calla Lily. The two djinn had risen and were hovering above their sarcophagi. Electrical charges sparked from Khalida's fingers, while Amani's hair lit up the moonlit sky and flickered in the water's reflection.

"I'm finished with you doing everything you can to destroy me and the ones I love. You want everyone to see who I am? Then let's finish this, Khalida."

Amani didn't wait for Khalida to respond, but instead cast the first blow. A streak of fire flew from Amani's fingers, hitting Khalida square in the chest, knocking her backwards. Unfortunately, the flames did not affect her in the slightest.

Khalida smirked, regaining her footing on the rocks. "You're pathetic. I thought you had more to give than that. This will be easier than I thought," she said as she used her power to lift the boulders scattered about and tossed them toward the Court members. "Stop that incessant chatting!" she shrieked.

Thoth managed to deflect them away from the group and snapped his fingers, hoping to bring the djinn to heel. It didn't work. "There is nothing I can do. I am disconnected from them right now." Confusion laced his every feature.

"Amani can do this," Calla Lily offered.

Overhead, the two djinn raged. Their powers met each other equally as they blasted one another with fire and sand, electrical bolts and

Khalida's new gift of ice. Their gold and silver hieroglyphs glowed brighter than the sun and moon combined. They stopped only for a moment, and in that brief flash, Khalida sent a shard of ice at Amani—striking her in the chest. Amani flew backwards, her hands gripping the frozen rod within her. She splashed into the pond, falling under its surface as Calla Lily and Nathan cried out. Thoth, Hathor, and Ma'at were huddled together, trying to figure out what to do next, when suddenly, the air became blisteringly cold. The goddesses and Thoth shielded themselves within a barrier, along with the jackals, Calla Lily and Nathan, but could only stand by and watch as Khalida turned the pond to solid ice.

"I can feel Amani beneath, but she isn't responding," Nathan cried out.

"And the baby?" Thoth asked Calla Lily.

"Her heartbeat is weak, but I can still feel her."

Seconds ticked away, and the chill in the air had frozen everything around them. Even the waterfall had been silenced by Khalida.

"This is only the beginning. When Amani's power is merged with mine, I will be unstoppable," Khalida taunted.

She had no sooner spat those words out of her mouth than her skin started to burn. The ice coating the ground beneath her melted into puddles. Khalida cried out, unsure of what was happening to her. Tiny fissures of gold began to replace the silver streaks beneath her skin. She was splitting open from the inside out. Khalida's body was hovering in midair, her white locks changing to black as everything that was ice was now becoming fire. The waterfall had once again begun to thunder and crash below, and Khalida was powerless to stop it as Amani burst from the pond to hover in midair.

"I said enough!" Amani raged, the silvery hue of the pond's water coating her skin. Her hair was not ablaze but there was fire within— something different. Amani was changed. Her skin was no longer dusky, but tawny. Her hair no longer golden and shimmering, but a mix of light and dark. Khalida tried to speak, but Amani clenched her fist, silencing her instantly. Amani was in control once again, allowing Thoth and the goddesses a chance to let down the protective barrier.

"You did well," Thoth said to Amani. "For a moment, it appeared as though Khalida was going kill you."

Amani did not reply, keeping her eyes on Khalida, but instead spoke into Calla Lily's mind.

Calla Lily touched Thoth's arm. "She did. The ice pierced her heart, but the aether in the water healed her. Strengthened her. She is changed, but unless you finish this, she and the baby cannot maintain control."

"Understood," he replied.

Hathor called out for her jackal guards, and they appeared instantly beside her. "Restrain that beast," she snarled.

The guards plucked Khalida from the air and placed her back on her sarcophagus. Thoth, Hathor, and Ma'at, all using a series of hand gestures, bound Khalida in place.

Once she was immobilized, Amani walked out of the water and lay back on the stone surface. "Please end this. For not only my child's sake, but everyone else's as well."

"I could never have predicted the strength of your union. I'm sorry the merging did not go as planned."

"Do not apologize. I never relished my power to begin with. It will be better suited for the goodness that lies within me."

"Very well," he relented, before looking over at Calla Lily. "When the power leaves Amani and Khalida, you should feel a surge within the child. Bind her. The age at which a djinn reaches maturity is twenty-five. It is not until then that we will know just what she will become," Thoth admitted.

Thoth lifted his hand, the watch Nathan had given him earlier appearing out of thin air, its internal mechanism in perfect syncopation with the baby's heartbeat.

"This belongs to the child. It is now part of her—connected to her through space and time. It will keep her safe and linked to all who love her," he proclaimed as he transformed it from a pocket watch into a locket. The chain of the watch had become a chain for a necklace instead, Thoth placing it on Amani and turning toward the goddesses.

Thunder and lightning roiled overhead as the three gods pooled their power to end the djinn who'd done so much damage over the centuries. The jackals held Khalida in place, and one by one they struck. First was Thoth, removing her Ren (name) and her Sheut (shadow). Second was Hathor, leaving Khalida without her Ba and Ka, her personality and vital spark. Lastly, Ma'at took her Jb (heart) and sent it to Ammit to devour. Khalida's body lay motionless before it dissipated into dust. Amani gasped, but when she opened her eyes, she felt the same as she always had in her heart and her mind. Nathan took his first real breath for the first time in minutes, and Calla Lily sighed in relief. The tension she had been feeling was now gone, and the baby's heartbeat was no longer erratic. They'd all survived—except Khalida.

Amani turned to Ma'at and Hathor. "What will our daughter be like?"

"That is unknown. She too is unique—part djinn, part human, and as of now, a bit of gypsy demon," Hathor answered.

"May I?" Thoth asked, reaching for Amani's arm. "I'd like to confirm a theory."

Amani nodded and watched as Thoth once again summoned her blood. This time, though, when it swirled in his palm, it was a trio of silver and gold mixed with copper. The copper shone and shimmered as the twisted ladder continued to levitate in his hand.

"Just as I thought. The baby's blood is the copper I couldn't identify before. Now it is clear."

"She is a mixture then of Khalida and me, as well as Nathan?"

"And Calla Lily. She is one of a kind for sure." He paused. "Remember you and Khalida were one and the same, split. Now you are reunited, and the other elements are from them," he said as he turned to Nathan and Calla Lily.

The ankh hovering in the sky above dissolved, and the Court all emerged from the ritual circle to look over at the group by the water. A lot had happened while they were protecting the perimeter, but they were clueless as to what exactly transpired except for the disarray of the area. They'd been too focused on their own task to know the specifics.

"Amani, Amani, Not Amani, Yet Amani," Tierri said in a singsong voice as the other pixie sisters joined her in the chant.

Amani gave them a confused look, reaching for her hair. "How is it that I look different? Is this the human side?"

Thoth shook his head. "There are no more sides, Amani. The parts of Khalida you were denied are now merged. You overpowered her and took back what was yours all along. Your djinn powers now reside within your child, making you fully human."

Roman and Mihail made their way over to the pond where everyone was now standing.

"Is everything okay?" Mihail asked as he took in Amani's new appearance. "You look well and healthy, and I hear the . . ." he paused, stalling his words.

"Why does everyone keep making cryptic comments? Hear the what? What are you not saying?" Roman demanded.

Amani eyed Roman. "I'm pregnant, and we didn't say anything until now because we wanted to be past the worst before sharing the good news."

Roman scoffed. "Another djinn?"

"Actually, only one now—her. I am no longer a threat, but neither is our daughter."

"Daughter! How could you possibly know the sex of the child? The baby couldn't be more than . . ."

Thoth interrupted to answer Roman's inquiry. "Because the baby's part djinn. That is why, and *she*," he emphasized, "will be none of your concern. We will be in charge of her well-being."

"And when can we expect you to be leaving Havenwood Falls?" Roman pushed.

"Seriously, Roman? It's been minutes, and you're already kicking them out?" Calla Lily snapped.

Saundra and Elsmed walked up to the group, with Irina and Madame Luiza only a step or two behind.

"They are welcome to stay as long as they wish," Saundra stated without hesitation. "Roman, you cannot decide alone who stays and who goes. We will convene a meeting and discuss this, but in the meantime, they may stay. Especially after what we have witnessed."

"And what exactly have you witnessed? We all saw the same thing. Us working magic, and this one," he pointed to Amani, "changing into something else. How do we know she's even pregnant, or that they didn't just merge one evil into another?"

Thoth and the goddesses started to speak, but Amani spoke first.

"How dare you," she seethed. "We will end this once and for all, Roman. That is, if you truly care to know the truth and not a made-up version of things."

"And how do you propose to show it to me, if you're changed as you say?"

Amani cast a glance at Thoth, who gave her an approving nod. "Give me your hands, and I'll show you."

Roman snatched her hands, gripping them in his own. "I don't trust you. Try anything, and you will pay."

Amani looked at Calla Lily and then over to Nathan before looking at Hathor, Ma'at, and Thoth.

"Watch closely," Thoth answered for her, "and she'll show you the way. Amani is human now, but for as long as the child remains within her, djinn power still surges through her veins."

Amani closed her eyes and splayed her arms out wide, letting the light within her build. The wolves came to stand by the shore, the pixies fluttered over the glistening water, and the Court all watched as a bright golden light radiated out of every pore in Amani's body. Everyone stared at her in awe as Amani's life—from birth to now— played out in a vision for all to see. When the last image appeared, they all could see the little bundle curled up and looking at them all. Nothing but peace radiated from her. She was perfect. She was strong, and she would be a formidable djinn when the time came, but for now, she was no more than the size of an apricot, and the proof everyone needed was finished being on display. The light dimmed, and everything went back to normal.

Amani sighed, and Nathan reached to hold her steady. He could feel how drained she was, and he stood by her side.

"I think you all have seen the truth. We are not here to hurt anyone, and I will tell you that it is not my or Amani's intention to stay in Havenwood Falls permanently. We believe we have other things to accomplish in this life, but until she is well enough to travel, we're asking for your blessing to remain," Nathan said, his voice unwavering.

"You have our blessing, Nathan. You and Amani are welcome to stay," Elsmed answered.

"Very good," Thoth said as he addressed the crowd. "It is time for us to return. Our work here is finished, but we couldn't have done it without your cooperation. If you're ever in need, you may reach out to me via Calla Lily. We now have a common interest to care for," he acknowledged.

Calla Lily nodded, and Thoth turned toward Ma'at and Hathor. "Shall we clean up?"

The two jackals lifted their burly arms and smashed the sarcophagi into dust before nodding at the goddesses and disappearing into wisps of sand. Thoth and the goddesses cleansed the area with a golden-hued smoke. As the air cleared, two flames emerged and Hathor and Ma'at stepped into the vermilion glow, disappearing into thin air.

Thoth walked over to Calla Lily and took her hand in his. "Another day?"

"Another day," she replied, a moment before Thoth vanished in his usual manner.

"Let's go home, everyone," Mihail spoke to the collective.

The group gathered their things and moved to head back into town. Calla Lily, however, stopped to pick up something she saw glinting in the moonlight.

"What do you have there?" Roman asked.

Calla Lily used her power to transform the blue glass bottle into solid brass before she turned around to face him. "Nothing but a simple decanter. They used it to hold some water to pour on the sarcophagus."

"Hmm."

"Can we go now?" She moved to leave.

"Of course."

"Still distrusting after all you've seen?" she needled.

"No, not at all," Roman said with a sly smirk as he stepped aside. "After you."

CHAPTER 16

*J*t had been a long night, and it was going to be another long day as everyone prepared for the "proper" wedding ceremony that would make things official between Amani and Nathan. Lillian was preparing to leave soon, and even though she wouldn't remember it, it was important to Nathan that she be a part of it, which spurred the urgency.

Ric served as the officiant, while Calla Lily, Irina, and Madame Luiza stood beside Amani in support. Everything was perfect. Everything was as it should be—as it was fated to be.

Lillian stayed a few more days, and then she took the train back to New York, carrying with her Nathan's letter to resign his teaching position. He and Amani would be staying in Havenwood Falls until after the baby was born. Then they would decide the best time to move on. They'd discussed perhaps visiting and even living in New York for a time, but eventually knew they'd most likely end up in Egypt, closer to Amani's roots.

As the days turned into weeks, Amani's pregnancy became impossible to conceal as the magically enhanced pregnancy continued to stun them all. The residents who had come to know her were all excited and joyous about the upcoming arrival. Amani, Tierri, and Ushka had used their gardening talents to spruce up the town square and every other available space where chrysanthemums would bloom. It was their way of adding some color to the world, and short of Roman, everyone loved the additions.

The air and the season shifted into fall, and Amani was glowing. Their daughter was anxious to arrive, as evidenced by the exaggerated kicks and movements. The cottage had become their home, and Nathan a welcome addition at the inn. He helped Mihail, Irina, and Madame Luiza with whatever was needed. He also worked at the library. He'd sent away for books and other miscellaneous items that might help the Court and the town.

Calla Lily, Nathan, and Amani had all agreed the day after the merging that the Prison of Asria needed to remain hidden. Amani could still recognize it, because the watcher's vessel always seemed to call to her. Now, though, Amani assumed it was not her the vessel was calling to, but the baby's djinn traits. The night Calla Lily picked it up by the falls, she read its intent, and without knowing the details of the images she saw, all she could do was hide it to keep it out of the wrong person's hands. The watcher's vessel now sat inconspicuously on a shelf in her house, alongside other decanters. Like the locket Amani wore around her neck that was linked to the baby, it was spelled with Shuvani blood and could not be broken or changed unless she was aware.

It was a crisp fall morning, and Amani was walking toward Callie's Trinkets and What Nots with a handful of blue water lilies—Calla Lily's new favorite flower—to meet her friend for lunch when her water broke. Amani gripped the flowers and her belly.

"All right. It seems you're hoping for a grand entrance," Amani said to the baby.

Nathan replied in her mind, *"I'm on my way."*

After a few hours in the privacy of their cabin, Qadira Nymphaea Caerulea Wade was born on November 22, 1920. She was healthy, happy, and above all, where she belonged. Nathan and Amani wanted to give her soul the same blessings Neema had given Amani on the day she was born—a name befitting her, a name to enhance the life she'd been given. Qadira meant powerful and capable, while Nymphaea

Caerulea, the scientific name for blue water lily, was an homage to the strong women in Nathan and Amani's lives—Lillian Hartman and Calla Lily Mircea. It was also to honor Thoth, Ma'at, and Hathor for all they'd done to make this moment possible.

Amani held Qadira in her arms and whispered, "You are my life, little one, and I will cherish every second I am given with you."

The floor of the cottage was instantly filled with a dozen or so bright blue lotus blooms—Egyptian water lilies—along with a papyrus of a woman holding a child to the sky. It was a gift from the heavens. A message that even when it seemed impossible, we could all rise up, find the sun, and be released from a curse.

EPILOGUE

*N*athan and Amani loved Havenwood Falls and hated leaving the peace and tranquility of it, but the time had come for them to move on. Qadira was now two and more curious than they ever could've imagined. She loved connecting to the magic of the Great Falls and playing with the pixies. Even the wolves and the angel took interest in the little djinn. However, the one person whose fascination she could never seem to thwart was Roman. To him, Qadira was something to study and watch. Amani always kept her close, but without powers of her own anymore, Amani was unable to know what his intentions truly were. Calla Lily suggested that the time was right for them to go to New York. Nathan had secured a new job offer, and they'd be in Egypt after the New Year arrived.

It was hard to leave the place they'd met, fell in love, changed, and had their daughter in, but it was for the best. Amani, while still pregnant with Qadira, had worked with Calla Lily and Saundra to create a way for the town to stay safe from outsiders, but retain their memories after leaving. They'd created a marking system inspired by the marks Amani and Nathan received from their binding that would allow the Court to track and monitor the visitors to the town. From that time forward, all who entered Havenwood Falls would be welcomed, with conditions for the supes—a mark specific to each that linked to the town's protection wards. And now that Amani was human, she and Nathan had no need to receive the marks, but the Court insisted on marking them as a way of keeping track of them— an insurance policy of sorts. Amani was a lovely person, but no one yet knew what powers she still held while pregnant, nor what the child would become. The tattoos would serve as the Court's hidden tracking.

Their tattoos mirrored each other, in the form of two ankhs wrapped lovingly in a pair of golden wings, but were also infused with a spell that would allow Nathan, Amani, and Calla Lily to maintain the communication link they had opened with their blood. For as long as Nathan and Amani lived, they'd be connected mentally with Calla Lily and Qadira at all times—no matter where they were. It was a failsafe Thoth and Calla Lily added during the merging. It, along with the locket, kept them all safe and in sync, should something arise with Amani or Qadira.

Calla Lily had blessed the locket around Qadira's neck and kissed her gently on the cheek. "Call to me whenever you need me, little one. I will always be here," Calla Lily whispered as they all said goodbye at the Montrose train station. Hugs and tears spilled as they bade each other farewell.

"I'll see you all when you get settled in Egypt," she said into their minds as the train pulled away from the station.

"Love you, Aunty Calla," Qadira replied sweetly.

When Calla Lily arrived back in Havenwood Falls, the town seemed quieter, emptier, but that was because everyone knew they'd never forget how a human, a djinn, and a very special baby girl had changed their lives forever.

We hope you enjoyed this story in the Legends of Havenwood Falls series featuring a variety of supernatural creatures. The series is a collaborative effort by multiple authors.

Lost in Time by Tish Thawer

Dawn of the Witch Hunters by Morgan Wylie
Redemption's End by Eric R. Asher
Trapped Within a Wish by Brynn Myers
Blood and Damnation by Belinda Boring
Fated Beginnings by E.J. Fechenda
Emeline by Katie M. John
Released From a Curse by Brynn Myers
A Pack of Lies by Kallie Ross
Kiss the Ashes by Desiree Lafawn
Hidden Truths by Colleen Nye
Wrath and Retribution by Belinda Boring
Changing Fate by Char Webster
Rise of the Witch Hunters by Morgan Wylie
The Drowning Bride by Seven Jane

Also try the main Havenwood Falls series; the YA line, Havenwood Falls High; the darker, sexier side of town, Havenwood Falls Sin & Silk; and the local supernatural college, Sun & Moon Academy.

Stay up to date at www.HavenwoodFalls.com

Subscribe to our reader group and receive free stories and more!

ABOUT THE AUTHOR

Brynn Myers is an adult paranormal romance author. After considering writing a hobby for years, she finally turned her passion and talent into a career. She came into the paranormal genre later than most, but has always loved fairy tales and all things magical. Using that love, she creates charmed worlds by writing stories involving passionate, strong-willed characters with something to discover.

You can find out more about Brynn and her all titles by visiting www.brynnmyers.com and subscribing to her newsletter at www.brynnmyers.com/subscribe.

ACKNOWLEDGMENTS

I'd like to thank Ang'dora Productions for letting me be a part of the Havenwood Falls crew again for part two of Nathan and Amani's story. I'm so grateful to be among the amazing authors in this shared world. I'd also like to give a special thanks to Kristie Cook for allowing me to use Madame Luiza, Mihail, Irina, and Saundra in some of my scenes. Randi Cooley Wilson, THANK YOU times a million for letting me tap into Calla Lily Mircea and bring her to life in these two stories. Amani is asking I keep the kudos for Roman to a minimum, though. LOL! Also a special thank you to T.V. Hahn's pixies, Kallie Ross's Ric Kasun, and E.J. Fechenda's Elsmed.

To Liz Ferry, I'm so grateful you're a part of the Havenwood Falls and Ang'dora Productions team. You're invaluable! Thank you for all your hard work and support.

Amber Leaf Publishing, thank you for your love and support in all my work. I will never be able to thank you enough.

To my readers and anyone new to www.brynnmyers.com—much love and gratitude!! Every time you pick up one of my stories and give my characters a chance to warm your hearts or royally tick you off, I am honored to be on your reading lists.

AN EXCERPT

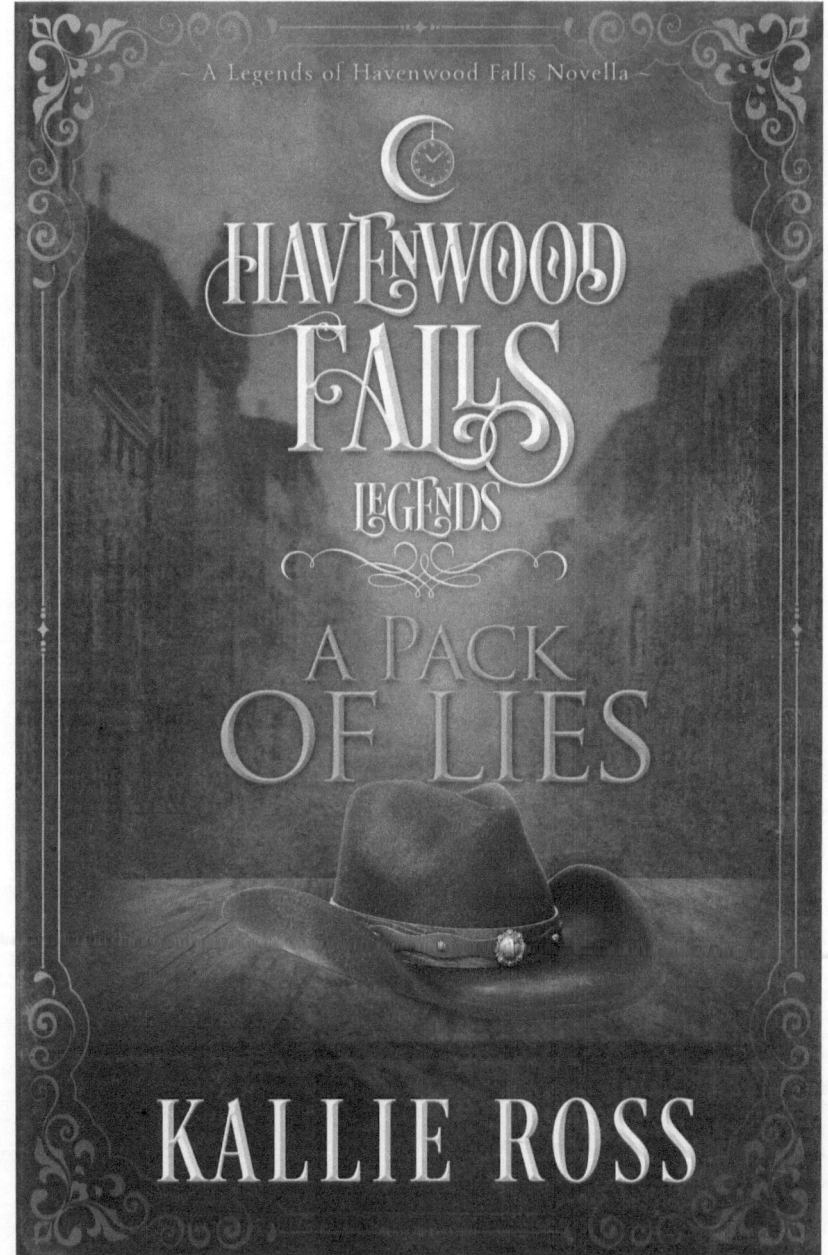

~ A Legends of Havenwood Falls Novella ~

HaVEnWOOD FALLS

LEGENDS

A PACK OF LIES

KALLIE ROSS

A Pack of Lies (A Legends of Havenwood Falls Novella) by Kallie Ross

Gaby Kasun, alpha of the Kasun Canyon Pack, is responsible for protecting her people and the magical falls hidden in the mountains in the Wild West. With the threat of war looming, hostile natives, and an emerging new world, she rules with desperate determination, while struggling to ensure her pack's survival.

In the summer of 1820, as the pack prepares for winter, Gaby receives a message of hope from an old acquaintance—promising wealth and security in St. Louis. All she has to do is travel to the big city, collect what the pack needs, and return home before the first snowfall. With no other options available, she and her mate Ric hit the trail, determined to turn things around for their people, no matter the risk.

When Gaby and Ric arrive at the gussied-up, gun-slinging city, they're met with obstacles at every turn. The Creole Elite, a group of tycoons led by Benedicte Trudeau, have other plans for Gaby. The alpha is forced to fight for her life as she battles to save her people and her relationship with Ric.

Supernaturals hidden in plain sight. Concealed love. A life-ending shootout. Gaby must unravel a pack of lies to save herself and her pack.

A PACK OF LIES

1860

"Momma!" Conall cried from his bedroom.

Ric and I looked at each other, me hoping he would offer to go check on our son. He shrugged. My mate stood in the kitchen over the sink, his hands covered in suds. We had fallen into a routine in the evenings. After tucking Conall into bed, I sat in the living room reading while Ric washed pots and pans.

"We'll have to teach Conall to do the dishes soon," I said with a smile, and tucked a ribbon between the pages of my book to mark where I'd stopped.

"I like that idea, and not only because it means I won't have to do them. My attention would be better spent on you after a long day of keeping the peace," Ric said, his voice low and flirtatious.

He winked at me and chuckled.

After he turned his attention back to his work, I tiptoed over to him and slid my arms around his waist from behind. He had changed clothes when he arrived home after work, but he still had dirt smudged across the back of his neck.

"If a traveler saw you right now, they might mistake you for a miner. It's been a long time since you've worked with a pickaxe, but you get just as dirty as sheriff. You need a bath as badly as that skillet," I teased, nestling my face between his shoulder blades.

"How about you go check on Conall, and I'll fill the tub?" Ric asked.

"Okay, but it's late, and chilly outside," I reasoned, knowing the trough we had in the back of the cabin would be private enough, day or night, but the temperatures grew downright freezing after sunset in the canyon.

Ric turned and held his hands out, so as not to get me wet. "I'm sure I could find a way to stay warm if you'd join me." He growled playfully and leaned down to kiss me.

His lips were full and warm to the touch, and gone again before I could explore them. I tried to pull him closer, but his frame was too wide and too strong. In a blink, he'd turned and started scrubbing the pans again.

My mouth fell open. "Wha—"

Ric interrupted, "You'd better go check on Conall before—"

"Momma?" Conall called innocently. He had gotten out of bed and was standing behind us.

"Oh, cuddle bug, let's get you back in bed." I turned to pick up our solid five-year-old. He was growing up too fast. His round face was becoming more square, like his father's, and his childlike faith was becoming more skeptical. I hated to admit it, but his cynicism had been inherited from me.

"Will you tell me a story?" he asked, with widened eyes and a pouty bottom lip.

I couldn't help myself. "Of course. Which one do you want me to tell you?"

"Don't be too long," Ric said, insinuating more than Conall knew, glancing over his shoulder and smiling at us both.

I giggled, and Conall waved a hand in the air, half delirious from exhaustion. Our boy had been at school most of the day, then ran errands with me in our growing community. Before six years ago, it had only been our wolf pack in the forest surrounding the falls. But in that short time, with the arrival of a party of supernaturals drawn to the magical water, the settlement had tripled in size.

Conall's room was small, but he spent very little time there. He preferred to be outside. His patchwork quilt hung haphazardly off the foot of his bed. When I sat him on his mattress, he laid his head on his pillow and waited for me to spread his blanket over him. He sighed thoughtfully as I sat down at the end of his bed.

"Momma, will you tell me about the time you went to the big city with Daddy?" Conall asked, and a yawn escaped him just before he finished the question.

"Um, sure, but why that story?" I wondered out loud and tucked his covers under his feet. Ric must have told him about our trip to St. Louis, because I had spent the last twenty years trying to forget it.

"Because I wanna go there someday and be just like Daddy. I wanna ride a steamboat, and be a gunfighter, and go to a ball," Conall rambled with a second wind of excitement. "And drink at a saloon, and play poker with cardsharps, and have a shootout, and save you from the bad guys, and—"

"Wait just one second," I told Conall, and held a hand up to keep him quiet until I could get Ric in the room. "Ulrich Kasun. You had better get yourself in here to explain exactly what you've been telling our son about St. Louis." I had intended to sound disparaging, but a chuckle escaped me.

I didn't have to yell, because like me, Ric had enhanced hearing. He heard me use his given name, and I expected him to enter the room with his tail between his legs. Ric and I had been on many adventures over the years, but there were certain things you didn't explain to a child, like shootouts.

"Yes, dear." Ric shuffled into the room with his eyes on the hardwood floors, wiping his hands with a small towel.

I cleared my throat, and he looked up. "What's this you've been telling Conall about our trip to the big city?"

"I merely told him the truth," Ric said, looking at Conall and avoiding eye contact with me.

"The truth, huh?" I asked with a little sass.

Ric shrugged.

"Sounds more like a pack of lies," I accused, and straightened my skirt.

Ric walked around Conall's bed and sat opposite me. "Well, then, I'd love to hear your version."

His challenge was accepted.

"This is what really happened . . ."

1820

The October sun had set the sky ablaze, bright orange and red at the plateau's horizon. Another dry, unseasonably warm day. I'd felt a tug at my chest, and knew Ric was close. Our connection alerted me to his return and provided an excuse to leave our dusty, loud settlement. The quiet place reminded me of a time when our pack wasn't concerned with progress. I had diligently watched for the scouting party Ric was in to return, hoping they would have new supplies in tow to help us through the winter.

As alpha, I could have assigned anyone to the task, but members of the pack had been bickering for weeks about how to deal with our shortages. Coming up with a plan to replenish our supplies before the first snowfall had been my number one priority. I explained we would have everything we needed. The land would provide. But, because of the drought, some argued we needed more. More food, more cabins, more blankets, more tools to mine for gold—their list went on and on, and I had grown weary trying to convince them to see reason. We had to keep our discovery quiet, or greedy settlers would flood the mountains.

At the top of the ridge, near our people's settlement in the forest, peace and tranquility had embraced me. We'd built half a dozen cabins, scattered safely in the forest, and learned to store supplies in natural caves along the canyon walls. From a distance, no one would have suspected a group of people lived in the area.

I lifted my canteen to my lips, and took a long drink. The sound of the falls in the distance had always reminded me that it would provide us with the water we needed, but I wondered if I could provide the leadership my people needed to carry them through to spring. Our forest was like a protective barricade from the outside world, but from inside, with dangerous amounts of snow and ice, it felt more like we were being held hostage.

Ric's mother, our last alpha, would have known what to do.

I closed my eyes and took a deep breath. The smell of burnt grass still overpowered the scent of new growth pushing up through the ash in spots across the plateau. The drought had ruined our crops, but nearby natives had set fires as a warning around the canyon to keep us away from their camps.

"There is nothing left for us here," Nina had said sharply. I'd heard her approach, and turned to find her wearing a long cotton dress and a frown. I thought she should have looked happier. Nina Novak and her husband, Peter, had convinced the pack to abandon our guise as a native tribe and build a proper settlement. The change in appearance had probably been the reason the Ute felt threatened. Our pack's progress made us look more like the people attacking them from the east.

"That's not for you to decide," I told her with conviction, and folded my arms over my chest.

I may have given in when it came to modern conveniences, but we'd held our ground on guarding the falls, even after the Ute tribe rode through and lit the plateau on fire. The neighboring natives had never attempted to invade our land before, but they were being driven off their lands because of war, and what the British, French, and Spanish called progress.

Nina placed a hand on my shoulder and said, "Adele might have chosen you for Ulrich, but she's gone. No one would blame you if you gave up your role as alpha to someone more qualified." She sounded haughty, and her nose tilted up in the air.

"You're right." I shrugged out of her grip. "*Ric's* mother picked me. But the magic in our blood chose to bring us together as mates. Adele understood and made her decision. You're just jealous because you weren't chosen to be either."

Nina hated my nickname for my husband. As Ric's distant cousin, Nina had been born with Kasun blood, alpha blood, but her tactics reminded me of the life we had left in Croatia over a hundred years ago. The Blood Lake Pack had become savage, and Adele's own brother made an attempt on her life.

Some died to get us to the New World, including Adele, but not before naming me as her successor. Our people had lived as humans, with the ability to shift into wolves, for thousands of years. The magic that ran through our blood also called us to our mates.

"Adele forced her will on us all, but without a daughter, your legacy will die," Nina mumbled bitterly and turned to walk away.

"Even without Adele's decision, Ric and I would have mated. You never had a chance with him, and your selfish motives would have us all dead if you were alpha." I bit the inside of my cheek to stop all of my anger from spilling out. The taste of blood filled my mouth.

Nina had been a thorn in my side since we were children. Her ability to hit a nerve and scurry off without apology reminded me of the vermin that threatened our food stores. The rats ate, gorging themselves, and left disease behind.

The hint of a vibration in the ground caught my attention. I turned and tilted my head, tucking my hair behind my ear to listen. My wolf's heightened hearing alerted me to the approach of two horses, with riders, and a wolf.

Something was wrong.

There should have been two horses and two wolves returning from the scouting trip. Nina must have noticed, too, because she froze. Her mate, Peter, had been a part of the group with Stephen Horvat, Boris Greg, and Ric. The four men had been best friends growing up, but the journey to the New World had tested their bond. After the fire, the men put all of their differences aside to find a way for us to trade for supplies.

Along the horizon, the silhouettes of two riders and a wolf had become more distinct. One man was draped over a horse's back in front of its rider. In a matter of seconds, I was able to make out Ric, a black wolf running at full speed ahead of the horses, and Boris and Peter in human form on horseback. It was Stephen lying limp over Boris's horse.

"Go!" I shouted over my shoulder at Nina. "Get Maria and the others. Meet us at our cabin."

Nina would want to check on Peter, but my alpha orders had a way of overriding any pack member's personal inclinations. I hated having so much power over the others, and rarely asserted it. Nina flinched. And without question, she nodded and proceeded to shift into her wolf form. Her dress, shredded, fell to the ground as she darted toward our settlement.

The next few hours were spent trying to stop Stephen's bleeding. He'd stepped into a fur trader's trap, and the iron contraption had nearly taken his leg. The men had been scouring the area for possible connections to trade. For several days, no one had appeared along any of the paths occasionally used by travelers.

Then Ric explained who'd shown up the previous night, and why Stephen had been so careless in their rush back.

With a low rumble, my mate's voice carried across the room. "A messenger on horseback appeared to have been riding for his life, probably scared of the natives. We waited in the tree line to follow him, but then he stopped and called out for you, Gabriele." Ric reached out and took my hand.

"He knew my name?" I asked, shaking my head in confusion. There were only a handful of people I'd revealed myself to in the New World, and Ric had always stood by my side when we encountered outsiders. "Did you recognize him?"

"No, I'd never seen the man before, but he clearly inspected the area before calling your name out. Like he'd been told exactly where to go and what to say. We all smelled blood, and knew he had to be injured." Ric looked over my shoulder to Peter and Boris. They nodded in agreement, and went back to tending to Stephen, who'd been placed on our bed. "After a few minutes, the stranger climbed down from his saddle. He was in bad shape, and stumbled to the ground, pulling his saddlebag with him."

I squeezed Ric's hand. "What did you do?"

"We waited for him to pass out. It seemed cruel, but it was the only way to make sure he would not ask questions or follow us." Ric slipped his hand out of mine and ran his fingers through his recently cut hair. "He was no trader, because there was no sign of a wagon or furs. Even though we'd taken measures to look like those traveling west, we had to protect the pack and the falls."

"I understand." I nodded, and placed a hand on Ric's arm. He shook his head slowly, struggling to say whatever it was he needed to tell me.

Peter Novak moved across the room to join us. "It is not your fault, Ulrich." Peter patted him on the back. "He could not be saved."

Ric shrugged out of Peter's grip. "We don't know that, because we waited too long," he gritted out, sounding irritated.

"He'd been attacked on his journey to us. What would we have done if he had lived, Ulrich? Send him back to St. Louis, knowing of our settlement? He would have sent others back to take what's ours," Peter claimed with an air of authority.

Since arriving in the New World, we'd encountered natives, explorers, pioneers, settlers, and once, time-traveling witches. The existence of supernaturals was no secret to a pack of wolf shifters, but protecting our secret was the only way we knew to protect our lives.

"Peter, I appreciate your reasoning, and agree with most of it, but do not be mistaken that we have any claim over these falls. In fact, the oath Ric and I took to protect them puts us in servitude, not ownership," I clarified, speaking across the room so the others would hear as well. I hated how Peter and the other men could manipulate Ric.

The Novak, Horvat, and Greg families had grown up with Ric and me in Croatia. We'd chosen to follow Adele Jezero, our alpha, to the New World when war divided our pack and led to the Ottoman

Empire taking over our homeland. Through the years, the other couples had begun having children while I struggled to learn how to lead our pack.

I was still learning.

"Of course," Peter said, with a hint of hesitation, and nodded. "You'll want to read the letter we found in the man's saddlebag."

Peter reached into the chest pocket of his coat and handed it to me. I glanced from Peter to Ric.

Ric shrugged.

"Thank you." I took the worn piece of parchment from him and recognized my name written across the front. The black wax seal had been broken at its edge. "Who's read its contents?" I asked curtly, annoyed that any of them would be so bold as to read their alpha's correspondence.

Ric glanced at Peter, then he looked over at Boris, who looked up from Stephen's limp form. I knew they could all read English, because I had taught them. For the first time, I regretted it. They all knew I could use my power as alpha to force it out of them, but instead I left the question open.

Silence.

I looked down at my feet and gritted my teeth together. The sound of boots shuffling on the hardwood floor let out a loud creak. I looked up to meet Ric's gaze.

"We wanted to protect the pack," Ric answered slowly, unsure of himself. I was convinced the others persuaded him to read the letter.

"Outside," I barked at Ric with anger. "The rest of you—" I exhaled, taking in the room. The four walls suffocated me. Our friends called it an advancement from the tepees we'd found shelter in in the past, but I found the cabin more like a cage.

I pushed past Peter and Boris, then turned to face them. "Make sure we don't lose Stephen."

The brisk cool night invited me with a crescent moon peeking through a canopy of trees. If I were not alpha, I'd have shifted and run through the forest surrounding our settlement. The thought reminded me of a time when I could do whatever I wanted without the responsibility of the pack.

My life in Croatia had been spent watching my parents and older brothers fight in support of Adele, the Blood Lake Pack alpha. She'd trusted her wolf pack, not using her magic to bend others to her will, but some took advantage of her trust. There were pack members who had believed Adele was soft. Our battle, fighting for freedom from those who were willing to expose our abilities in exchange for power, was only one in a war that took all my family. Adele had been quick to invite me, a devastated ten-year-old, into her home. Her husband, Matthias, had become a father figure, and their daughter, Nikola, was a best friend. It was her son, Ulrich, whom I struggled to connect with, and it was not until ten years later, on our journey to find a place in the New World, that I understood why.

Ulrich had always been stubborn and quiet. He consistently fell in line with what his friends wanted to do. I relished the days he kept his distance. He infuriated me whenever he called me black sheep, because he said I was too kind to be a wolf.

Somehow, after a few months of traveling through rough terrain and missing home, I realized he had become my home.

My heart had grown to love him, and the magic running through my blood called to him. As is our custom, Ric took my surname when we married. He revealed that he'd been in love with me since the day his mother introduced us and explained I would be a part of their family. Only, Adele had not known at the time it would be as Ric's wife, and not as his adopted sister.

I paced.

Sensing Ric, I didn't want to be mad at him, but his constant attempts to protect me made me feel weak. He hadn't meant to undermine me, but I wasn't sure if Peter had the same good intentions. Ric leaned one of his broad shoulders against a nearby trunk and crossed his arms over his chest.

"What do you want me to say?" Ric asked, wanting to fix the problem before he even knew what the problem was. "I'm not sorry we read it. Otherwise, we wouldn't have rushed back so quickly."

"*We*," I growled. "*We* is you and me. I am insulted you included Peter, Boris, and Stephen, before I was able to determine if they needed to know my business."

I huffed and turned my back to Ric. Looking at his handsome face would only make me more conflicted, even if he wasn't remorseful. I carefully unfolded the paper in my hands and slowly read the words scribbled on the page.

June 12, 1820

> *Dear Gabriele Kasun,*
>
> *I hope my personal messenger has found you well. He has been ordered to protect my message with his life. Since our last encounter in New Spain, my trade business has brought much fortune. It would never have come to fruition if it were not for your daring rescue.*
>
> *I traveled safely back to Louisiana Territory, now known as Missouri Territory, without any altercations with natives or bandits. My family has settled in a town along the Mississippi River called St. Louis. In fact, delegates have approved a proposed state constitution to establish a state of Missouri in the near future.*
>
> *Your hospitality and generosity have not been forgotten, and it would be my pleasure to host you as my esteemed guests at my estate. My wife, Marie, hopes to show you her appreciation for saving my life in person. Our children are also eager to meet the brave woman who fought off a pack of wolves and mended my injured arm without a hint of a scar. Sometimes I think they don't believe me, so you must visit and prove them wrong.*
>
> *Your beautiful furs and precious metals would be welcome for trade, and are handsomely sought after in our parts. It would be my pleasure to broker for any supplies you may need to endure the coming winter. The name Chouteau has grown more well-known since we last met. So follow the map below, and when you arrive in St. Louis find the nearest trading post and ask for me.*
>
> *I look forward to repaying your kindness,*
> *Auguste Chouteau*

I looked up from the thick, creased parchment, and Ric searched my face. My eyes widened at the prospect of providing for our pack, but I knew why Ric was defensive about reading the letter.

"This might be the only way we all survive through the winter," I said, waving the letter in front of Ric.

"*Might?* It is the first week of October," Ric said with raised eyebrows, and took a step closer to me. "You won't have time to get there and back before the first snowfall. The falls must be protected. What if you're kidnapped, or someone discovers your magic? What if you don't return at all? I won't let you go." His jaw flexed, and he propped his hands on his hips, making him look more like one of the walls of the cabin.

I glared at Ric until a man's throat cleared.

"You have no authority over her decision," Peter said.

Peter pushed a tree limb to the side and planted himself next to me. The move was uncharacteristic of Peter. I made a mental note, but took advantage of his support.

"What he said." I folded my arms over my chest and nodded in Peter's direction. "Besides, Chouteau will be close to sixty by now. He will pose no threat."

"Why is he reaching out to you now?" Ric asked with suspicion. "Why wait so long? He must have an ulterior motive."

"I'm sure he does," I agreed, remembering his ability to sweet talk me into helping with his fur trade so many years ago.

Auguste Chouteau had been a young fur trader when we first met, and he had happened into our territory late at night. Out of supplies himself, and desperate for food, he spotted smoke from our fires. A wolf patrolling our borders, Stephen Horvat, attacked him without provocation.

As a wolf pack, we've always been connected, and when in our wolf form, we have the ability to communicate thoughts to each other. Stephen had mentally pushed a call of distress out to the rest of us, and by the time I'd arrived, Chouteau had been in danger of losing his arm.

The irony of Stephen lying on my bed with a similar leg injury was not lost on me.

After ordering the pack to retreat, I approached Chouteau in my human form. In disguise as a native tribal woman, I wore animal skins with my hair tied back in long braids. Chouteau had as much reason to fear me as he had the wolves, but calmly pulled out a bag of gold coins and begged for assistance.

After I had nursed him back to health with medicinal herbs, Chouteau and I agreed to trade furs for supplies. He returned to the region annually for eight years. Eventually, I shared news of our settlement discovering some precious metals—small nuggets of gold, and a rare red gold. I sent him back with some of the metal and he returned with more supplies than we could have needed in two years combined.

After those eight years, I had to cut ties. He'd innocently complimented me. Chouteau remarked on how young I still looked, and I knew any future trade would result in more questions than I could honestly answer.

But thirty years later, we needed supplies for winter, and fast. We had mined more gold over the years, and even discovered another vein of the red gold Chouteau liked so much. I had a feeling it would trade better than furs.

Facing Ric, I mirrored the stern look on his face. I knew what I had to do. My word as alpha would be final. Magic would bind my orders to the pack. I had to make sure my words would also protect them.

Ric suddenly placed a hand on my cheek, stopping me, and whispered, "I'm going with you."

Purchase *A Pack of Lies* where books are sold.